M000085961

DOMNALL

Immortal Highlander, Clan Mag Raith Book 1

HAZEL HUNTER

HH ONLINE

✦✦✦

Hazel loves hearing from readers!
You can contact her at the links below.

Website: hazelhunter.com

Facebook:
business.facebook.com/HazelHunterAuthor

Newsletter: HazelHunter.com/news

I send newsletters with details on new releases,
special offers, and other bits of news related to
my writing. You can sign up here!

Chapter One

A drop of rain plopped on Jenna Cameron's face, rousing her from a sleep so deep she felt muddled. She saw trees, sky, clouds. Huge trees. Dark sky. Gloomy clouds. As she regarded her surroundings shivers sprinted over her wet, chilled skin. Nothing looked familiar, and yet she felt a tremendous relief pouring through her. She had done something. She had reached something. Her thoughts felt remarkably peaceful, as if she hadn't a care in the world now.

She never wanted to move again.

Wind came rushing through the trees, fluttering the leaves and creaking the branches. Pine and rain scented the damp air moving over her face. Everything around her felt soaked, from the wide, hard rough thing pressing against her back to the mound of things under her cheek.

Not things, leaves.

She felt her heartbeat speeding up as she tried to understand what was happening to her. All she knew was her name: Jenna Cameron. She didn't know where she was, how she got here, or who had done this to her. She took in a quick breath and tried to recall anything else, but her mind felt wrong. A sharp, tight cord of pain began to twang slowly between her temples. Had she taken a blow to the head? She couldn't remember.

All she knew about herself was her name. How was that even possible?

"'Twill be well, lass."

Those four words drew her gaze to the mountain of a man standing over her. Jenna wasn't afraid of him. It simply confused her to discover him there. From his expression, as he crouched down in front of her, he seemed just as bewildered.

Jenna liked his eyes. A beautiful shade of green, they tilted up at the corners, giving him a slightly feline look. Gold tipped his dark lashes, and caught the sunlight as it sifted through his long brown hair. He had very striking features, broad and bold and intensely masculine. Under his dark cloak he wore a rough, oddly-made shirt, wool trousers, and fur-topped boots.

"Domnall mag Raith," he said, his deep voice colored by a heavy accent she didn't recognize.

It took her a moment to understand that he was telling her his name. "I'm Jenna Cameron. Where am I?"

"Scotland."

That wasn't very specific, but at least it put a name to his accent. She eyed his heavy belt and the sheath that hung from it. He had his left hand curled loosely around the hilt of what had to be a sword. When he saw her staring, he let it go.

"I'll no' harm you," Domnall said, as he took off his cloak and covered her with it.

Until he did that Jenna hadn't realized she was naked. The warmth of his cloak felt so good she wanted to burrow under it and never come out.

They went on looking at each other, in a

cautious, startled way that made her think of
two accident victims who had just climbed out
of their wrecked cars. Was this his fault, or
hers? Jenna had no idea.

At last he asked, "How came you here?"

"I don't know."

Worry invaded her comfort and started
issuing demands for information. How long
had she been out here in the woods? Had
Domnall brought her? Hit her over the head?
Was that why she couldn't remember
anything? Why was she in Scotland, of all
places?

The wet, cold ground felt as uncomfortable as all those questions she couldn't answer.
She needed to get to her feet.

Domnall saw what she meant to do and
took gentle hold of her arms, helping her up.
As they both stood Jenna saw just how much
he towered over her. Her head barely reached
the middle of his chest. She glanced down at
her feet as he wrapped his cloak more securely
around her. She wasn't that short. He was
simply huge: broad shoulders, big arms, long
legs, and bulging muscles everywhere. His
hands covered most of her upper arms. If he

wanted to hurt her, she was a goner. Right now, she should get busy with screaming, crying or shouting for help.

Why aren't I afraid of him?

"Jenna Cameron." He said her name slowly, as if it belonged to a language he was trying out for the first time. "'Tis a Scottish name, but your voice."

"American." She said it without thinking, and then smiled. "I'm from America." There was something else, too, something important hovering just behind that. It made her head hurt to reach for it, but finally she dragged it out of her dark memory. "I'm an architect."

Phantom sensations came over her as the fact brought with it fragments of memory. Water lapping over the toes of dirty boots. A groaning, cracking rumble roaring overhead. Then terror, bright and piercing, running and falling, being struck over and over by huge, heavy blows. Agony, despair, and then in that terrible darkness, light from above. Cold, glaring white light, and snowflakes falling on her face…

Jenna pressed one hand to her head, gasping as her headache swelled. Just as suddenly it vanished, and the terrifying memory bits went with it.

"I'm in trouble," she told Domnall. "I think someone tried to hurt me. Maybe kill me." She clutched his cloak, trying to draw it tighter around her shivering body. "They must have left me here."

Jenna glanced around them, and that was when she saw the marks on the huge tree trunk just behind her. She turned around slowly, her stomach clenching as she took in the long row of marks that had been burned into the tree's bark. She couldn't read the primitive glyphs but they looked very familiar. They also made every muscle she owned tense, as if readying her for a fight.

"Do you ken what they mean?" Domnall asked.

"I've seen them before, but no."

She reached out to touch the marks, and at the last minute snatched back her fingers. That made his cloak slip from her shoulders and drop to the ground.

"Be still, lass," he said when she bent to retrieve it.

Jenna felt his hand on her back, and then

her eyes closed as pleasure spread from the stroke of his fingers along her spine. "What are you doing?"

"You've skinwork here from your neck to your waist." He traced the pattern for another few seconds before he picked up the cloak and wrapped her up again. "By the Gods. 'Tis the same."

"As the tree?" she asked as she turned around, but the big man shook his head.

He hesitated before he pulled up his left sleeve, revealing his hard-muscled arm. A long tattoo of the glyphs in black ink ran from under the fabric to his elbow.

"'Tis the same as my own."

⚜

FINDING A NAKED, unconscious female in the very spot where he had awoken twelve centuries past gave Domnall mag Raith much to think on. Seeing she had been inked with the same glyphs as he bore on his arm added to the mystery. That Jenna Cameron could no more remember what had happened to her than he had upon his awakening suggested

she'd also escaped the grove of stars. Yet she
offered no more answers than he had when
Galan Aedth had brought Domnall and his
men out of darkness.

'Tis naught more to be done.

Only the druids knew of the grove of stars
and its ways. Domnall had to take the lass
back to the settlement. Behind his back he
signaled to the four other defenders watching
them from their positions around the ash
grove, and faint shuffling sounds answered
him as his men retreated.

To Jenna he said, "I must take you to our
headman, Galan Aedth. He's a powerful *dru-
wid*, and may aid you in remembering."

"Okay." She glanced down at her bare
feet. "Did you see my shoes?"

She'd come to the enchanted forest as
naked as the Mag Raith had, and he doubted
she could walk in his boots. Domnall didn't
want her pretty feet torn by the rough trek
they'd have to make, so he scooped her up into
his arms.

Jenna made a surprised sound, and curled
her hands around his neck. "You don't have to
carry me."

"Aye, but I think I must, lass." He'd be hard-pressed to put her down again, too.

As he carried her out of the grove Domnall thought of his cottage, hidden deep in the woods, and the wide, comfortable new bed he'd made himself last spring. The tribe's goose tender had saved him enough feathers to line the straw ticking. He imagined her in it, wrapped in one of his blankets, waiting for him. Her slight weight and soft skin pleased him as much as the scent of her, like a rose blooming under the stars. It had been too long since he'd taken a lover, but the sweet, gentle tribeswomen who offered him and his men comfort in truth preferred their own kind.

What would Jenna offer him?

Naught. Why such a thought had come into his head, Domnall couldn't fathom. *She's in need of help, 'tis all.*

Her fine skin and delicate features made him wonder if she might be a *dru-widess.* He'd never heard of magic folk dwelling in America. Where could such a strangely named place lay? In Britannia or Francia? He knew so little of Scotland beyond the Moss Dapple's boundaries it might be a newly-named land within the old borders. The only thing that seemed familiar was her very dark hair, similar to that of the Cornovii tribes to the south—if they still flourished. Doubtless much had changed since the days when he and his men had freely roamed the highlands.

He'd never seen such eyes. They looked blue in the sunlight and violet in the shadows. The color reminded him of the panay flowers that bloomed near springs and streams.

"You should stop and rest if you get tired," she said, her bright gaze shifting over his face with open curiosity.

She spoke as if she were an ox and he a stripling. "I dinnae grow tired, lass."

Carrying her to the settlement required Domnall to skirt some traps he and his men had set for a wild boar that had grown troublesome of late. It also gave him some time to ponder how he would approach Galan. Since his great falling out with the headman, Domnall had kept his distance to avoid another skirmish. He'd never felt any particular liking for the *dru-wid*, but he and the other hunters owed Galan their lives. Serving the headman and his people as their defenders allowed them to repay the old debt as well as give them purpose.

Some of the Moss Dapple's bairns came running to stare at Domnall as he brought Jenna into the center of their settlement. Because they had isolated themselves from the rest of the world, the tribe lived simply but happily in their forest. It provided for all their needs, and they in turn nurtured it to sustain their tribe. Though none of the Mag Raith could remember how they had come here, Domnall and his men had been mostly content among the Moss Dapple.

Yet the Mag Raith were not *dru-wid* kind, and never would they be.

"Domnall," Jenna said, drawing his attention from his thoughts. She sounded wary now. "Please put me down."

Carefully he placed her on her feet, and adjusted his cloak so that it better covered her bare body. When she had awoken in the forest, he'd averted his gaze from her nakedness. Before her pretty eyes had opened, however, he'd looked his fill. She had beautiful skin, as creamy as churn milk and as smooth and unmarked as a newborn's. She possessed the flat belly and boyish hips of a young lass, but her full, high breasts assured him she'd left childhood behind her. He never imposed himself on any female, but keeping his hands from touching her had proven a surprising struggle. The possessiveness of her, to which he had no right, refused to leave him.

Now that he'd held her and carried her Domnall regretted bringing her to the settlement. He might have hidden her in his forest cottage for a time. There he could have talked with her, and gleaned any memories she might have of the grove of stars. Jenna might even remember how she'd arrived there, and shed light on some of the darkness in his past.

"Overseer," a low, tight voice said.

Domnall's remorse doubled as Galan Aedth approached him and Jenna. Taller and broader than most *dru-wids*, the headman wore richly-worked green robes adorned with the tribe's forest symbols. The sight of them stirred his anger, for his storm-gray eyes had darkened to match the flat blackness of his hair. His temper, of late uncertain, would surely burn high again if the severity of his expression was an indication. As Galan was the most powerful *dru-wid* among the Moss Dapple, that promised nothing good.

"Headman," Domnall replied. He inclined his head as a show of the respect he no longer felt for the man, and took a discreet step closer to the lass. "I found this lady in the ash grove. She's called Jenna Cameron."

"Indeed." Galan's eyes narrowed as they shifted to the lass's face for a moment, then he regarded Domnall. "Why dinnae you wear your armor, or carry your axe?"

The *dru-wid* would have him sleep in his defender garb if he could.

"The men and I went to set snares for that boar plaguing the gardeners." To draw Galan's attention from yet another contentious matter between them, he gestured behind the lass's back, indicating the length of her skin-work. "Jenna's marked as we were, and hasnae memory of her ordeal."

Galan's upper lip curled. "Or so she's told you. You've no reason to place your trust in this wench. Likely she was sent to distract you while her scheming masters plot to siege our lands."

A low laugh came from Jenna, who shook

her head. "I'm sorry. Scheming masters? You can't be serious."

"Dinnae speak to me, outsider." Galan's jaw tightened as he glared at Domnall. "Take her to the cider house and confine her there. I shall consult with the Gods as to what 'tis to be done."

Chapter Two

As Jenna walked through the settlement with Domnall she saw sympathy in the eyes of every person she passed. She also noted how different they looked compared to Domnall. None seemed especially tall or muscular. Their narrow faces, gentle eyes and delicate builds made them seem almost fragile compared to the overseer. They certainly didn't make her feel as unsettled as Domnall did.

She also couldn't understand why a bully like Galan had become their leader. To have such an angry man in charge of a peaceful village seemed like a terrible match, not to mention his bizarre talk of scheming masters and their plots.

Past the outskirts of the village they took a trail that led to a wide, low wooden structure constructed of heavy logs with saddle-notched corners. The cider house appeared well-maintained, and the sharply-peaked roof looked as if it had been newly-thatched. Looking at it brought a sense of seeing something incredibly old, like some rare artifact. Nothing about it invoked any memories of her home or the buildings in it. Neither had any of the tribe brought back a recollection of her own people.

Only Domnall seemed familiar, although she couldn't put her finger on why. Nothing about him prompted any associations at all. His clothing seemed strange to her, and the sword he carried almost bizarre, as if she'd never seen one, which seemed unlikely. She'd also swear she'd never seen him before in her life. Yet the inexplicable sense of knowing him wouldn't leave her.

"You don't belong to this tribe, do you?" she asked, still studying the structure.

"No. My men and I awoke here, as you did, in the ash grove. We were hunters before we came here." He stopped and glanced back over his shoulder, shaking his head once before he regarded her. "I must leave you now."

He didn't sound happy about that, Jenna thought, any more than she was. An aching hollow expanded in her chest. "Do you have to lock me up? I promise I won't hurt anyone or run away."

"The Moss Dapple dinnae permit outsiders on their lands. You shouldnae be here." At the door he turned a latching bar and eased it open. "I'll speak to Galan again."

The smell of sweet, ripe fruit came pouring out of the dark interior. Jenna saw the outlines of a large, primitive press and tall baskets filled with apples and pears. At least she wouldn't starve to death while the men decided what to do with her. She stepped over the threshold, and then turned to look at her savior.

Don't leave me alone. That thought bothered her, but not as much as the next one that popped into her head. *Come into the dark with me.*

"Forgive me, lass," the overseer said before he locked her inside.

෯෮෯

DOMNALL USED an old trail leading from the cider house to walk to the orchards, where he'd sent his hunters to await him. He signaled them to follow him to his cottage. None of the men spoke as they filed inside and gathered near the hearth. He went to the woodpile for a split of juniper to toss on the glowing embers before he regarded the other Mag Raith.

"I've locked Jenna Cameron in the cider house, as Galan bade me." And he might never forget the stricken look she'd given him as he'd closed the door in her face. "He didnae welcome her when I brought her to the tribe. He accused her of serving masters who scheme to take our lands."

Mael, Domnall's tracker, shook his head. "That dreary fack's gone crazed again. Next, he'll order you take her head, and then I shall break our vow and—"

"Guard your tongue," Edane said and went to the window to glance outside.

The reminder that his archer no longer felt safe in speaking openly, even away from the settlement, added more weight to Domnall's doubts. Edane had always been sensitive to the moods of others, and often of late seemed deeply disturbed by the headman's increasingly zealous nature.

"By the Gods," Mael said. "Dinnae tell me you believe Galan's blethering. She's but a wee lass, left helpless and fearful." His topaz eyes narrowed as his gaze shifted to the archer. "You drew closest, Brother. Did she stink to you of enchantment?"

"She smelled of rain," Edane replied as he tugged absently on one of the thin, bright red braids he'd woven in his unruly mane. "I felt naught of magic from her. I reckon she's no' come to do harm to us or the Moss Dapple."

"You cannae claim thus," Broden said, his handsome face as cold as his rasping voice. "The finest lures dangle soft and sweet and helpless."

"So speaks the master trapper," Kiaran said and gave a comforting scratch to the neck feathers of the small, agitated kestrel perched on his shoulder. The raptor immediately calmed. "I stood too far to see much of the lass, but she didnae behave with treachery. More like wholly bemused to my mind. Would she no' have attacked you, had enemies sent her?"

Domnall considered all he'd sensed from Jenna, as well as the startling similarity her plight bore to their own.

"She's no' evil." He met Broden's narrow gaze. "You didnae see her when she woke. I saw in her eyes the same as I felt when we first came. No memory of how she'd landed there. The skinwork on her back, 'twas done in the same fashion as ours. 'Tis near a match for my own."

None of the Mag Raith had ever remembered what had taken them, marked them and then discarded them. Their second lives had begun on the day they'd awoken in the Moss Dapple's forest after being rescued from the underworld by Galan. Whatever had captured them had removed their Pritani ink completely, along with the battle spirits that had once guided them. The *druwid* had claimed that only the Gods had the power to do such things. Since none of the Mag Raith could remember a moment of their ordeal, they had accepted his explanation.

Now Domnall wondered if the headman had told them all he'd known.

"She's a brave one," Mael said, ending the stretching silence. "No' once did she weep or rail at her predicament. Few lasses have such courage."

"She doesnae seem to me Scots or *dru-wid* kind," Edane said, sounding thoughtful. "Her words, some confounded me. I've no notion of what 'architect' means." As the other men muttered in agreement, he glanced outside. "We've to patrol soon. Mayhap we should decide our path before enraging the headman anew."

"The lass cannae live on apples," Mael said. "She'll want a proper meal, and some warming brew."

"Garments and shoes as well," Kiaran said. "Galan shallnae permit the tribe to provide them to an outsider. She's nearer your size, Edane."

The archer sighed as he looked down at his lanky body. "Aye, torment me again on what a fine wench I'd make."

"Mayhap we should take turns to spoon-feed the poor lass," Broden said sourly, folding his arms. "Then cobble her boots and sew a fine gown. Edane may beseech the Gods to favor her. Aye, why no' we all pledge loyalty to the wench?"

Mael scowled back at him. "She's a dove, you great thick-skull, no' a wolf."

"Or she's a wolf in dove's feathers," the trapper countered. "Mayhap architect means 'devourer of men's hearts.'"

Edane gestured toward Broden's chest. "If she's that hungry, we'll feed yours to her. You've no use for it."

"At least *I've* one," the trapper countered.

"'Tis no fathoming this for now," Domnall declared. He didn't want his hunters' bantering to escalate into a quarrel. "Edane, fetch something for the lass to wear before you go on patrol. Mael, round the cider house, then join him. Kiaran, stand sentry at the settlement, and keep watch on the headman. Listen for my signal. We may want to move quickly."

"And me?" When Domnall eyed Broden, he folded his arms. "I'm Mag Raith, no' a tree lover. Bid me do, and I shall see 'tis done."

His trapper might nag like a fearful old

crone, but in the end, he always remained loyal.

"I'll want you at the river entry," he told him. "If the *dru-wid* decides against the lass, I'll take her out to the nearest village. All of you, listen for my signal."

"You'd defy the headman to see the lass saved?" Broden demanded. "When you ken naught of her?"

Every word rang true, and yet not. Domnall did know something of Jenna. He'd felt that in his bones since the moment he'd spotted her in the grove. Like so much that had happened to him and his men, he could not put a name to it. He didn't have a single memory of her, and doubted they'd ever met. Still, he knew he had to protect the lass until the truth about her could be revealed.

"I ken she's as Galan found us, our minds empty and our hides branded by the gods," he said finally. "She's lost all her memories, so she cannae even speak to her tribe. She's no one but the Mag Raith to protect her, and that I shall do." He scanned their faces. "What say you, brothers?"

"Aye, Overseer." Mael thrust his fist out. "Mag Raith *gu bràth*."

The other hunters echoed him as they added their fists to the tracker's, forming a wheel of arms.

Domnall reached out and covered their fists with his broad hand, sealing the agreement. "Mag Raith *gu bràth*."

Chapter Three

Futility and fury dogged Galan Aedth as he retreated into the privacy of his cottage. As headman of the Moss Dapple he had labored for more than twenty incarnations to obtain an elusive prize. In vain, even he would admit, for he had come no closer to obtaining his heart's desire. The arrival of Jenna Cameron once more pushed his face into the ever-steaming pile of his own failure.

Yet this wench might provide him with a new chance to crawl out of his own *cac*.

Shedding his outer robe, Galan strode to the small, windowless chamber at the very back of the cottage. The cold, heavy air within smelled of the meditative herbs he'd burned the previous night in a wasted effort to restore his balance. He went to his alcove to study the focal stones and crystals he kept there. Most had grown dusty from lack of use, but the power they contained yet shimmered in their depths. He selected a broad, flat-sided chryso-lite the color of curled, new leaves, and carried it to the spell circle in the center of the chamber.

The cairn stele he'd built for his castings contained stones gathered from dozens of sacred oak groves. Long ago Galan had discovered a secret that he'd kept to himself. Over the millennia the stones absorbed some of the magic from the portals. Using such stones increased his own power tenfold, and enabled him to become one of the most formidable spell-casters among all druid kind. As soon as he placed the chrysolite in the niche atop the stele its depths brightened. After kneeling and beseeching the Gods to aid him in his quest, Galan focused on the crystal.

"Show me from whence this female calling herself Jenna Cameron came."

The yellow-green surface of the crystal

grew clouded, the murky grayness burgeoning and darkening. Yet as Galan watched nothing clearly showed. Just as nothing had every time he'd tried to see into the past of his Mag Raith defenders. Only fogginess, and then blackness as the crystal went dark.

"'Tis the grove of stars that took her?" he asked. "Please, I beg you, help me see."

When not a flicker of light reappeared, he seized the crystal and threw it across the chamber. It bounced off his meditation chair and fell to roll lazily back to him, rocking back and forth as if to say no.

The Gods ever deny those who would demand of them, lad, his old trainer had told Galan in his first incarnation, when he'd indulged in a youthful fit of temper. *You must entreat, entreat, entreat.*

He dragged in deeper, slower breaths until his resentment subsided. Bowing to the ground, he pressed his brow against the floor boards.

"Forgive me my ire. I would only ken what I must to protect my tribe."

That was a half-truth, one of many he'd told the Gods since discovering the Mag Raith

hurled naked and unknowing into the Moss
Dapple's enchanted forest. Since that day
Galan had struggled in vain to solve the
mystery of what had happened to the hunters,
and yet had found not a trace of the truth.

Now this wench had appeared, speaking in
that strange accent and looking as if she'd
been bathed in milk and massaged with
perfumes every day of her young life.
Claiming herself to be an American, when no
such country existed, and an architect, which
he knew to be utterly ludicrous. But he
shouldn't have accused the wench of treachery. The overseer's cool eyes had filled with
contempt for him—again. Keeping his hold
over the Mag Raith required them to feel they
owed him their service. Domnall's sense of
obligation waned each time they clashed,
and soon—

A timid knock came at the chamber door,
and when he jerked it open the young druidess
standing outside took a quick step back. He
looked over the novice, whose dark red hair
and pale brown eyes indicated she was one of
Aklen's brats. He would have to speak kindly

to her, or the tribe's shaman would again have hard words for him.

"What do you want of me, Sister?"

"My sire bid me bring you a calming brew, Master Aedth." Her hands shook as she extended the steaming cup. "Might I prepare your evening meal?"

Had it grown that late? Galan had lost track of the hours. "No, Sister, but go with my thanks to your sire." He took the cup and shut the door.

Aklen had been meddling much like this of late. It annoyed Galan that he could barely control his own people anymore. Keeping the Mag Raith subservient to him much longer already seemed unlikely. Domnall had openly refused to obey his orders more than once now. If the overseer decided to abandon his vow to protect the Moss Dapple, Galan would never discover what had given the Mag Raith their extraordinary abilities as well as their unique nature.

He now had no doubt that the five Pritani had been changed by some great, unknown power. But how? What had been done to them had not come from druid kind. Of that Galan was convinced.

Domnall and the hunters could heal from any wound, no matter how grievous. During long winters when food had grown scarce, they'd given their shares to the tribe's children, and yet never suffered from starvation or sickness. Each hunter also had been given a unique ability that provided him startling power, yet wholly unconnected with magic.

Nor did any of them seem to age.

That such simple-minded brutes possessed what Galan had so long coveted never failed to cease chewing at the headman's gut. He gulped down Aklen's brew, scalding his tongue and throat. The pain felt distant compared to the envy burning in his soul. Reincarnation required him to wait for his new form to mature, a tedious interval. Thus far he had always come back from the well of stars, but he dreaded the yawning darkness between each lifetime. If he had what the hunters possessed he need never surrender to death. He could at last find the means with which to bring back that which his cursed son had stolen from him at birth.

Fiana.

For his dead love Galan would learn the secrets of the Mag Raith, if he had to drag the hunters and Jenna Cameron into the afterlife himself.

Chapter Four

J enna had listened to the heavy sound of Domnall's footsteps as he'd walked away. She didn't want to be left alone, but the big man would be back. She simply had to be patient. As for this nameless attraction she'd developed for him—a man she'd met barely an hour ago—it was probably due to whatever trauma she'd suffered. Yes, of course it was due to the trauma, and the fact he was big and kind and strong, and had those beautiful feline eyes in such an arresting face. He probably made every woman indulge in secret fantasies of being alone with him, and stroking her hands over that magnificent body and all those beautiful muscles...

Enough of that. You don't even know him.

Picking up a small, red-gold apple, Jenna walked around the press. The wooden components of the crude mechanism had weathered to silver, but appeared clean and well-maintained. Rows of empty barrels in various sizes had been neatly stacked to one side, along with rolls of rough-woven hemp. Several troughs also stood ready for use. She envisioned the cider house workers collecting the leavings to feed them to the livestock after the fruit had been pressed.

How do I know what they do with it? I'm an architect, not a farmer.

That could mean that she'd come from farming people, or lived near a small agricultural community.

Light filtered in through some slits in the wall too narrow for Jenna to squeeze through, but the straw covering the dirt floor looked clean. She spotted a pair of large leather gloves that would definitely be too big for her, a stained apron hanging from a peg, and a set of wooden clogs. A quick check revealed the shoes were a fit. Slipping them on, she sat down and took a bite of the apple, which flooded her mouth with tarty sweetness. Suddenly hungry, she ate every bit down to the core, and then dropped it in one of the troughs. Her sticky hand made her grimace, but she didn't see any water she could use for washing.

Would Domnall keep her here for hours? Days? Why had Galan treated her like an enemy? What would make him think she could be one?

Jenna blew out a long, shuddering breath. All she had was questions and nothing to do but wait. She leaned back against the wall and forced herself to close her eyes. Though she wasn't tired, she was just beginning to realize what she did feel: overload. The more she thought about it, the more everything around her felt wrong. The buildings, the people, and even the forest didn't seem right. That had to be because she didn't belong here.

As for where she did belong, she felt completely disconnected from it, as if she hadn't fit there either.

"I'm an architect," she muttered.

Going back to the one thing she knew about herself made her feel a little more at

ease. She was an architect, which she knew
meant she designed buildings. Judging by her
recognition of the cider house's features, she
at least knew how to build house-size wooden
structures. She studied her hands, which
appeared small but nicely shaped, with short-
trimmed nails and calluses in a few spots. She
rubbed her thumb against the hard patch on
the side of her middle finger. She must work
with her hands a lot, drawing things to be
built, yet nothing she'd designed came back
to her.

Maybe she wasn't an architect. She could
be pretending to be one. *Sure, for my scheming
masters.* Galan's zany accusation made her
laugh a little. *What is that man's problem, anyway?*

Time passed at a slow, uneasy crawl. As
her patience finally ran out, Jenna got up and
went to the door, leaning against it to listen for
any noises outside. As far as she knew she'd
only technically trespassed on the tribe's lands.
If Domnall and his men had done the same
thing, then why weren't they locked up with
her? None of this made sense. She needed to
get out of here and find out what had
happened to her. As that last thought ran

through her head, she felt her hand against the door grow warm, as if she held it over a stove.

As she stared down at it, her fingers turned opaque and sank into the wood.

"*No.*"

Jerking back, she stared at her hand and then the door. Her fingers shook as they returned to normal. Gingerly she flexed them, and turned her hand over and then back again. She let out the breath she didn't realize she'd been holding.

"What the…"

She balled her hand into a fist and glanced at the door. Her head told her that what she'd just seen was impossible, but the surge of adrenaline coursing through her body told her to do it again. She flexed her fingers one more time, and they seemed the same as they ever had. With a small nod, she squared herself to face the door. Slowly she touched her fingers to the wood.

Watching them, she felt the warmth in them spread to her palm and then down into her arm. She pushed, and her hand changed again and went through the wood, followed by her arm to the elbow. She froze as she felt wind brush against her skin. Her hand and forearm were on the other side of the door.

Closing her eyes for a moment, Jenna let the warmth engulf her. Her body followed her arm, passing through the wood. A heartbeat later she stood outside the cider house.

"Wow."

She turned around, her body growing even warmer as she stepped back through the door into the cider house. On the other side she staggered a little, her knees shaking as if she might collapse. She stood still until the shakes passed and her panicked breathing slowed. Sweat trickled down the side of her face like hot tears.

Pressing her palm to her forehead, Jenna could hardly believe how very warm she'd grown, as if she were running a low-grade fever. Her back felt uncomfortably hot, too. If she kept using this bizarre power of hers, she suspected she'd keep heating up. Pushing herself through the wood created some kind of friction.

I'll only do it one more time.

Instead of trying to walk through the door

again Jenna retreated to the back of the structure, where she waited for a few minutes. As she suspected her body began to cool down. When the feverish heat faded away, she took a deep breath and pressed her hands against the wall.

Before she could blink, she stood outside again, Domnall's cloak swirling around her in the wind. She leaned back against the wall, shaken. This ability definitely felt new.

All around her the forest stretched out in every direction. The sunlight streamed down from a now cloudless sky.

Where do I start? Who do I trust?

Domnall's handsome face flashed in front of her, but he couldn't help her, not when his headman wanted her kept locked up, or worse. If the tribe found her wandering around they'd probably turn her over to Galan. She couldn't rely on anyone but herself, and somehow that was a very familiar situation. Going back to where this had all started seemed the most sensible choice. Something in the ash grove might give her an idea of why this had happened to her. Gathering the cloak around her, Jenna broke her promise to the big man and headed into the woods.

IN THE FOREST Mael slipped through the trees, stepping on roots and grass where his passage would make no sound and leave little trace. From long habit he kept to the shadows as cover, concealing himself wherever he could. He moved with such skill and care that he passed within a hand span of a pair of grouse intent on mating without disturbing their courtship.

"Hide your nest well, little *máthair*," he murmured once far past them. "Our doltish headman may decide you're hatching wee spies."

Mael had learned to walk a silent path long before he'd gone on his first hunt. As a small lad he'd learned that eluding Fargus mag Raith, the brute defender who had sired him, had been the only way to escape undeserved beatings. Fond of belligerence, bellowing, and bloody brawls, Fargus worked off much of his endless wrath by beating his mate and their children. The larger Mael had grown, the less he'd had to endure his sire's fists. Like any *burraidh*, Fargus had been a coward who preyed only on those who could not possibly hurt him.

Quiet and thoughtful by nature, Mael had been sickened when he grew to be the image of his sire. Most of the tribe assumed he'd inherited the man's hateful temper as well. Once he'd reached manhood, he stood even taller and broader than Fargus, and others had begun moving out of his path when he approached. Then his sire had injured his shoulder and could not serve as a defender, which combined with too much drink at the evening gatherings stoked his temper even higher. Not a night went by that Fargus did not beat his mate and daughters.

The looks of pity from those who knew how his sire behaved in private infuriated Mael. Nothing could be done about it. Among their tribe a man's family was his to do with as he pleased. Mael had no right to challenge his sire, and would be punished harshly if he ever tried.

With his injury Fargus could no longer

hunt, and so it fell to Mael to provide for his family. He never took pleasure in the kill, but being able to escape the settlement allowed him a few hours of peace. He and Domnall rode out so frequently they often encountered each other in the hills, and in time began hunting together. Mael's natural gift for tracking paired well with Domnall's lethal speed with spears. Three others joined them, and with their skills the five Mag Raith were soon able to provide for the entire tribe.

Things did not improve, however, when one night Fargus broke his youngest daughter's jaw, and his mate's arm.

In the weeks that followed Mael became adept at taking down the vicious tusked grice, a huge wild swine known to attack rather than run from hunters. Every pig he ended provided preparation for what he knew he had to do. Fargus would never hurt anyone again. All Mael allowed himself was to go on one last hunt with the others before he brought down condemnation on his head.

Instead he'd brought down the very wrath of the Gods on him and his four friends.

Since that day Mael had accepted that the

fault for what had happened to them lay on his shoulders. That he'd been obliged to become a defender himself seemed an especially cruel punishment from the Gods for his wicked intentions. Yet he served, grimly determined to redeem himself however he could.

Yet I'm to do naught while that facking dru-wid *names this poor lass an evil-doer, and locks her away.* Mael ducked under an oak bough to get a view of the cider house. *I should release her. I could fetch a horse from the stables, and guide her through the falls.*

He wouldn't, of course. Even if Galan burst into flames Mael wouldn't waste a piss on him, but his loyalty to Domnall remained as steadfast as the highlands. The overseer had done more than keep the Mag Raith sane through what had been utter madness. He'd made them brothers. Mael also knew that sending the lass off on her own without provisions or protection to be virtually the same as breaking her neck.

Too lovely.

Jenna Cameron didn't stir his passions—he ever feared hurting females as small as she—but her rare beauty troubled him. The first

man to see her beyond the enchanted forest
would claim her at once, whether she wished it
or not. Then her life would become as his
mother's had been, nightly servicing her
mate's uncaring lust and bearing a new bairn
each passing year. Mael would rather end the
lass himself than know she suffered the same.

A sharp whistle came from the route they
patrolled, reminding Mael of his other task.

Edane's waiting. Get on with it.

Two large villages might have occupied the
space between him and the cider house, but
still Mael could count the knot holes on its
logs. He also spotted a shimmer in the air just
behind the back wall. Such spelltrace could
not be seen by any hunter but him or Edane,
and he tensed, assuming the headman to be
the source. Yet a moment later he saw Jenna
step out of the shimmer and gather Domnall's
cloak around her.

"Oh, lass," he murmured, fascinated and
appalled. "What do you now?"

Her expression grew stubborn, and she
squared her shoulders before she walked into
the trees.

Mael watched her long enough to judge

her intent, and then altered his own path to track down the overseer. That he would say naught to Galan was already decided. The daft druid would only twist it to his own end. But did the overseer need to know? The wee lass had a rare courage, but bravery alone was not the same as protection. Mael nodded to himself. He would simply report what had happened: she had escaped.

Chapter Five

❦

Once she'd gotten out of the cider house Jenna knew better than to go ambling blindly through the forest. She didn't know how large it was, or if she could find an alternate route to the grove where she'd awoken. Instead she circled around the settlement, always keeping sight of it on her left, until she found the trail Domnall had used. She followed it directly back to the cluster of ash trees around the leaf-carpeted clearing.

Here we go.

For a few minutes she stood at the fringes and studied the site. No tracks other than Domnall's showed on the patches of ground between the trail and where she'd fallen. The glyphs on the tree trunk appeared black, as if burned into the bark, but the woodsmoke she smelled came from the direction of the settlement. The trees stood too close together for even a small horse to squeeze through them. She didn't see any drag marks her body might have left on the ground, or tracks her assailant might have left.

How had she gotten here?

Tilting her head back, she noticed some small branches on the marked tree. They hung from jagged breaks. On the ground below them more newly-broken bits were scattered among the tree's roots. The damage extended up as far as she could see, some sixty feet above the ground, but all in the same general area, as if something had fallen onto the branches and snapped them.

Me. I must have done it.

She reached into the cloak and touched her ribs and belly. There was no tenderness or swelling anywhere. No, she couldn't have fallen into the grove. From that height the impact would have shattered bones. Nor could she have walked in and collapsed. Her feet and shins would have been covered in mud and leaves. That left Domnall, who hadn't behaved at all like an abductor.

Or magic.

She might have laughed over that thought, but she'd just walked through a door and a wall. Yet even her new ability couldn't solve this puzzle. If she'd fallen into the grove in her ghost-form, she wouldn't have snapped all the branches.

Watching the ground closely, Jenna went to the marked tree. She saw the faint indentations and disturbances in the leaves that showed where her body had been. Closer inspection of the tree trunk revealed that the glyphs had not been burned into the wood, but carved and painted or inked with an indelible black substance. Once more looking at the esoteric marks made her body stiffen. She glanced down to see that even her hands had bunched into fists.

Whatever the marks meant, they weren't good. They made her head hurt. They made her want to hit the tree until her knuckles bled.

"'Tis the work of the Gods," a deep voice said from behind her.

Jenna closed her eyes for a moment. Though she hadn't heard Domnall approach, it somehow didn't surprise her that he had found her here. Slowly she turned to face him. Patches of sunlight shifted over him, threading bright amber through his thick brown hair and turning his green eyes to peridots. The shadows bold-lined his features as if to emphasize his masculine perfection, as if she needed reminding what a striking man he was. Everything about him pulled at her as if he'd cast an invisible lasso around her, and was slowly reeling her in. She had no reason to feel that way, but she didn't want to fight it. She needed to give in to it, to tell him, to put her hands on him.

Go to him. Show him what you want. He's waiting for you.

The crazy things bouncing through her thoughts made her think of Galan's accusations, and abruptly cooled all the desire looking at him had generated.

"I can't say," Jenna finally said, annoyed by how husky her voice sounded. She cleared her throat. "But I do know that I'm not working for evil, scheming masters. Are you?"

His gaze shifted back to the tree before he met her gaze again. "I serve Galan, and he's a man you shouldnae cross or defy."

He sounded worried. No matter what hold the headman had on him, she suspected that Domnall was at least sympathetic to her situation. "Your way of telling me that I should have stayed locked up in the cider house until you came for me."

"Aye, and 'tis still locked." He held out a bundle of folded clothing on which rested a pair of leather slippers. "For you. I'll want my cloak back."

Jenna crossed the clearing and accepted the pile, which turned out to contain a pair of lace-up trousers and a long-sleeved tunic, both definitely male in design.

"I was expecting one of those robes the ladies in the settlement wear."

He moved his broad shoulders. "'Twill no' please Galan to see you garbed as a *druwidess*."

Jenna made a circling gesture and waited, but he didn't move. "Would you turn your back, please?"

"When last I did, you escaped," he said blandly.

"Suit yourself," she said, matching his tone.

Since he'd already seen her naked it seemed silly to object to dressing in front of him. Removing his cloak and tossing it over his shoulder, she stepped out of the clogs and tugged on the trousers. They proved to be too big, but she tied the laces tight enough to keep them from slipping down over her narrow hips. The tunic also seemed huge as she shrugged into it, but all she could do with that was roll up the sleeves.

When Jenna glanced up, she saw that rather than enjoying the show Domnall had his eyes on the marked tree. The proof that he was a gentleman at heart made her wish they'd met under far different circumstances.

"Do you know anything more about those glyphs?" she asked.

"As much as I ken of how you freed yourself." He met her gaze. "'Twas a canny trick."

One she was going to keep to herself for the time being, Jenna decided. He probably wouldn't believe that she could walk through walls anyway.

"What happens to me now? Back to the cider house?"

He shook his head. "You'll want a meal. Follow me."

Because the apple had barely dented her hunger, and she doubted she could outrun Domnall, Jenna walked out of the grove with him. This time he took her down a different trail that led deeper into the woods. He didn't try to chat her up, which she appreciated. It gave her a chance to memorize landmarks.

The tribe's forest looked incredibly old and yet seemed bursting with life. Most of the trees soared high above her head, with trunks so wide she suspected they were hundreds of years old. Their leaves festooned every branch in heavy swaths of dense green. Birds sang and then chattered and squawked as she and Domnall disturbed them, some swooping low enough for her to see their feather colors and patterns. She didn't recognize any of them. For a second, she saw a pair of shaggy, red-colored deer grazing in the brush. A moment later they arched their heads, showing broad racks of velvety-looking antlers. Dark eyes glittering in their gray faces, they bounded away.

The trail ended at a small but thriving garden that had been fenced off, likely to discourage the deer from raiding it. She touched the braided vines knotted around the fence posts before she peered over to inspect the crops. She saw herbs and cabbage, and several types of squash and beans. Too small to be for the tribe, the garden had to belong to the overseer.

The thought of a man as big as Domnall gardening should have seemed comical, but instead it charmed her. "You grow your own vegetables?"

"Aye." He reached over and, with a dagger, cut a handful of herbs. "I've a fondness for them."

Beyond the garden they walked through another grove of close-grown pines, and then Jenna saw what they protected. The cottage looked much bigger than those she'd seen in the settlement, with a high thatched roof and sturdy stone walls rounded at each corner. Big windows covered by wooden shutters flanked a heavy hide and wood door, which Domnall simply pushed open. The threshold had been made high enough for him to pass through without ducking his head.

Inside Jenna stopped and took in the overseer's large front room. Handmade wood furnishings, carved with simple yet pleasing designs, occupied some of the space. Irregular-shaped gray stones had been flattened and fitted together for the flooring, their black and white streaks reminding her of old marble. One huge chair sat before a big stone hearth. On the speckled stone mantel stood carvings of animals. He'd left a bowl of fruit and half a loaf of dark, rustic-looking bread on his dining table, around which she counted five chairs.

Although Jenna saw no sign that anyone else occupied the cottage, he might not be unattached. There had been plenty of pretty women among the tribe, and he was an ungodly attractive man.

She tried to think of how to ask if he were involved, and finally came up with, "Do you have a family?"

"They're gone." He carried the herbs over to a primitive-looking kitchen area and added them to a lidded pot, releasing a delicious fragrance. "Come and sit."

"Can I help you with this?" She walked over to join him at the stove.

"Aye." He nodded toward a cabinet. "We'll need bowls and cups. Spoons in the flat box beside the platters."

Jenna retrieved the dishes and utensils, all of which had been made from carved wood and polished to a glassy smoothness. Setting the table felt as strange as watching the big man stir the pot on the stove. She must not be very domestic in her own life, or perhaps she lived with someone else who did such things.

What would it be like to live with a man like Domnall?

His cottage felt quiet and cozy, and she had the sense that it provided a sort of haven for him from all the responsibilities he had. The tidiness of the place definitely resonated with her, so she probably lived the same way. An image of curling up with him in a big bed under a pile of blankets made her smile a little. With him she'd never shiver again on a cold night.

A sudden thought made her smile slip.

What if I'm already with someone?

She didn't feel as if she were, and that had to mean something. If she'd been in love before she'd lost her memories, wouldn't she now feel a sense of loss?

Jenna noticed he was watching her, and wondered if her presence made him feel uncomfortable. He seemed like a man who would prefer being alone, which prompted her to ask, "Why don't you live in the settlement with the tribe?"

"I and the other Mag Raith arenae *dru-wid* kind," Domnall said as he brought the pot over to the table. "We're Pritani."

That name didn't ring a bell, but then, nothing did.

"Where are your people?" she asked as he ladled a thick stew from the pot into their bowls.

"Long dead," he said, and then went to retrieve a tall pottery jug with a cork in it. From it he poured a cloudy amber liquid to fill their cups. "From the cider house."

She took a small sip, and grimaced over the powerful sweetness of the fermented drink. "Whew." Carefully she set aside the

nk I'd better eat something before I
ore of that."

Domnall sat down beside her and sliced
the bread, giving her a thick piece before he
started eating. Jenna did the same. The herbed
stew, made entirely from vegetables, tasted
unfamiliar to her. She found it delectable,
especially when she dipped her bread into it as
Domnall did. They ate together in a comfortable silence, but she shook her head when he
offered her another helping.

"No room for more," she assured him.
"That was delicious, thank you."

He sat back in his chair, his bulk making it
creak a little. "You hold your *wheesht*, Jenna
Cameron. You're quiet, and calm," he added
when she frowned.

"Everyone here seems to be that way," she
pointed out. "Except your headman."

"For all that you've endured you've no'
wept nor shouted. I've seen caution in you, but
no anger or fear." Domnall gestured at her
arms, which she'd tucked loosely around her
waist. "Even here alone with me, you're at
your ease."

She couldn't deny that. "Should I not be?"

"Some moons back I met a lass who spok words strangely, as you do. Emeline McAra." He paused and watched her closely. "She came here with a shaman from the Skaraven Clan. Galan's son, Ruadri, as it happens."

Jenna realized he was expecting her to react to the names. "I'm sorry, but I don't know them, or if I did, I've forgotten them. Could they help with finding out who I am?"

"Galan wouldnae welcome them back. Indeed, he ordered me to kill his son." Domnall's mouth thinned. "I refused."

"That's horrible." Suddenly she didn't want to go anywhere near the headman. "Why would he want you to murder him?"

"This forest, 'tis warded against intruders. No outsider may trespass on Moss Dapple land. Except Galan's son, and his lady." He nodded at her. "And now you, lass."

WATCHING Jenna's face yielded no clue to her thoughts, Domnall decided. The lass had more than the gift of quiet. Her self-control rivaled his own and that of his men. Yet when the vicious order Galan had given

_used her surprise and dismay even

_re she spoke. He also guessed her to be quick enough to understand his meaning for confiding in her.

"Will Galan order you to kill me, too?" she asked, confirming that.

"I cannae tell you," he admitted, "but 'tis possible. Only ken that should he command me thus, you and I shall leave the tribe's lands."

"Or I could go now." She got to her feet and looked at the cottage door. "I'm ready. You just have to point me in the right direction."

Again, she spoke without fear, but decisive determination. If she had been a man Domnall would have called it *tapachd*. He'd never known a female to have that particular kind of courage.

"'Tis but one passage to the outside of the forest, and 'tis guarded." He rose from his chair. "Galan hasnae bid me harm you. Until he does—if he does—then I'm obliged to follow his commands."

"Why?" Her expression grew bewildered.

"Domnall, I'm fairly sure that I didn't choose to come here. I have no reason to trespass. All I've done is wake up in the wrong place. I'm willing to leave, right now. Wouldn't that make your headman happy?"

"'Tis more to it than you ken." Without thinking he reached out to her. "Forgive me, lass. 'Tis a wretched—"

The moment he took hold of her hand they both went still and stared at each other. Every thought drained from Domnall's head as a darkness enclosed them. All around them storm clouds swelled and flashed white from jags of lightning. Jenna's body glowed as if she had been wrapped in sunlight. His own half-naked body bore streaks of red blood and black gore. They floated together in that space, like two birds riding a strong wind current.

Don't make me go.

You cannae stay.

Domnall swept her into his arms, the light enveloping him as he held her close. In that moment to release her seemed unbearable, impossible. He'd rather gouge his own heart from his chest. He felt Jenna yanked from his embrace, and then he stood back in his cottage with her, as if none of it had been real.

"What did you, lass?" he demanded.

"No," she whispered, pale and shaking. Jenna stumbled back from him as she pressed her hands to her temples. "I can't. Don't make…me go…"

Domnall lunged forward as her eyes rolled back in her head, and caught her just before her head struck the stone floor. He lifted her limp body against his chest and carried her over to his hearthside chair, sitting down with her. Her skin had gone cold and damp, and her breathing shallow. The suspicions that Broden had planted in his thoughts abruptly faded. Anyone could deceive by word or deed, but the lass couldnae feign such a swoon.

She'd also used the same words as he'd heard in the vision.

He felt none too settled by it. The Mag Raith had dwelled among the Moss Dapple since awakening in the ash grove. Whatever had been done to take away his memories, he recalled every day he'd abided with the tribe, and his life among his own people before the last hunt. He'd never before seen Jenna until this day. The vision felt so real it had to be true, but it could not be.

Unless 'twas taken from us.

Domnall touched her brow and then her throat, feeling the soft throb of her heart in her veins. During their hunting days Edane had ever served as their healer, but he'd sent the archer to patrol the tribe's boundaries with Mael. Keeping her warm until she awoke was all he could do for now, unless she grew worse.

Settling her so that she lay against more of his chest, he watched the flames in the hearth. He never indulged in such idleness or much pondering. Long ago he'd given up trying to fathom what had happened to him and his hunters before Galan had rescued them.

Unlike Jenna he remembered his life before the darkness had swallowed him. Being the only son of Nectan mag Raith, his tribe's headman, had never been easy or especially pleasant. His sire had expected him to take his place someday, and had trained him ruthlessly in the countless responsibilities of ruling their large, affluent tribe.

Ye'll no' bring shame to this house, stripling.

Nectan expected his son to be first among all Mag Raith boys in strength, speed, and agility. On those rare times that Domnall had failed to please his sire, the headman would punish him harshly. He'd been forced to carry stones twice his weight up the slopes, or swim from one end of the loch to the other while bearing another lad on his back.

A man doesnae complain. We leave that to the females.

At first his sire's sternness had bewildered Domnall, especially when he saw the affection other men openly showed for their sons. Nectan had never once uttered a word to him in kindness or praise. If Domnall spoke out of turn his sire would answer with a sharp clout. Being subjected to Nectan's harsh demands had gradually hardened Domnall. In time he became the strongest, fastest warrior among the Mag Raith, and first choice as the tribe's next headman.

That he despised Nectan as much as the heavy yoke of prospective leadership had been known only to Domnall's hunting companions: Mael, Edane, Broden and Kiaran.

After boyhood the five of them had begun

hunting together to escape the village and their troubles. Mael, whose cruel, drunken sire wielded a heavy hand with his mate as well as his offspring, had been the first to join Domnall. Edane they had found one day practicing the bow in secret, a skill forbidden him, as he'd been in training to become the next shaman. During their hunts they also discovered Kiaran taming wild kestrels in the woods. He had been taken in by the Mag Raith after his own tribe had been slaughtered by Norsemen.

Kiaran had brought to their party another outcast he had befriended: Broden, the surly, silent son of a neighboring tribe's headman. Grim whispers abounded about the handsome lad, who had been sent as an infant to be fostered by the Mag Raith. This after his sire's wife had tried to garrote him, some said, but no one knew why. The deep scar around his neck bore mute testimony to the rumor, but his harsh, unfriendly nature kept anyone from confirming the facts. Even Domnall felt curious about Broden, whom he'd never seen speak to anyone.

"My sire got me on his bed wench,"

Broden said suddenly one day after they'd made camp, his belligerent expression daring a response. He had the rough, rasping voice of a much older man. "She bled out after my birthing, and his mate didnae care to coddle a slave's pretty whelp. Thus." He flicked his fingers at the scar.

All of them had gazed back at him, unsure of how to reply until Domnall said, "'Ye're the best trapper I've ever ken, but pretty?" He shook his head.

"He's no' so hard on the eyes," Edane added, tossing another split onto their fire, "yet I reckon I'm far comelier."

Mael nodded. "'Tis a sad truth. All the young lasses tag-tail after our archer, sighing and wishing to stroke his fine braids."

"When they're no' simpering over yer great wall of a chest," Kiaran put in, and pressed his hand to his chest as he let his voice rise to a feminine pitch. "Oh, Tracker, ye're so manly. Bond with me and sire my ten bairns."

"I'd sooner mate with one of yer wee screechers," Mael told him.

Broden had said nothing more, but after

that day he no longer dwelled in dour silence when among them.

Despite the trapper's blunt confession, they never again spoke of his luckless parentage. All of them carried their own pain and loneliness, and recognizing that in each other bonded them closer than blood ever might have. Hunting became their passion, and soon they devoted every spare minute to riding out together to chase game. In time they became the finest hunters among the tribe, and provided such bounty for their people that even in the cold, dark season no one went hungry anymore.

All of that changed when invaders came marching up from the south, hunting the magic folk and slaughtering any Pritani who crossed their path.

On the day they'd left the village for the last time Domnall had seen the distant storm heading for the highlands. For his own reasons he decided to chance it. Then Mael had spotted a bachelor herd of red stags, which had led them a merry chase. The herd had vanished in the thick woods surrounding a small, sturdy fortress. The storm broke over them, and hail had driven them to take shelter. Leaving the horses where they stood, Domnall had led his men inside the fortress...and had woken up in the Moss Dapple's ash grove.

"You're the Mag Raith hunters," Galan had said later that night, after Domnall had related what he could remember. "The five of you became legends."

"Became?" Broden asked.

"Before the Pritani died out, they told your story across the highlands." He met Domnall's gaze. "'Twas the invaders. The Mag Raith and their allies banded together to fight them, but the enemy didnae cease coming. In the end all of the tribes fell beneath their cursed swords. Thank the Gods my ritual offering in the grove of stars brought you out."

For the debt they owed the *dru-wid*, and the dismal prospect of having no tribe to return to, Domnall and his men agreed to abide with the Moss Dapple. Serving as their defenders gave some purpose to the rest of their lives, which passed peacefully. They protected the tribe as the years went by, but with time another strangeness became apparent.

The hunters never grew older.

The five remained young and strong, never growing sick, able to heal from any wound. Galan told them that they had been blessed by the Gods, and the tribe accepted their defenders without question or complaint. Domnall suspected their gifts had not been bestowed as a reward—far from it. For twelve hundred years he'd kept his own counsel, never putting words to what he suspected. The preservation of the brotherhood, the only family they knew, meant all.

But now had come Jenna.

"Don't make me go," she murmured, rubbing her cheek against Domnall's chest.

He gazed down at her, relieved to see the flush of color that had returned to her fine skin. With a gentle hand he brushed a sleek dark tress away from her face.

"I darenae make you stay, lass."

"Overseer, we must speak." Galan stepped through the door and regarded them both as if he'd caught them naked and facking. "By the Gods, Domnall. Have you gone mad?"

Chapter Six

Huddling in the darkness, Jenna waited for the light. It would come, and soon. Promises had been made. The pact had to be kept. She'd given her word, and no matter how much it cost her she had to keep it. She felt miserable instead of hopeful. She'd found hope. Now she had to toss it away and jump into the abyss.

If she didn't, none of them would ever escape.

Something cranked, slowly and heavily, and a solid shaft of white light rammed through the blackness. Now she could hear the sounds of fighting, growing louder with every passing moment.

She had to get up. She had to jump.

The clouds parted, their electric dampness crackling over her as she approached the ledge. Every step made her legs shake, but when she glanced over her shoulder, she saw the vague outlines of the others running toward her. They'd been found out.

No more time. She balanced on the edge, looking down at the river of cloudy air funneling beneath her. This could save them all, or kill her. Maybe both.

Jump. Time. Jump. Time.

Jenna woke up in shadows, kicking and thrashing. She hit something that made a heavy thump, and watched as dozens of apples rolled around her feet. She quietly groaned. It was the cider house.

Domnall hadn't believed her, or didn't trust her.

Or maybe I never left, and hallucinated the whole thing.

She stood up and righted the basket she'd knocked on its side. Her hands shook as she picked up the apples that had spilled from it. When she felt steadier, she walked over to the door and tried to open it. It didn't surprise her to find it bolted again. Domnall had picked his side. Taking in a deep breath, she shoved her hand through the wood, groped until she found the latching bar, and turned it.

Not a hallucination.

It felt colder than before and the sky overhead had gone a deep shade of violet. She must have been unconscious for most of the day and still they'd locked her up. She smelled smoke and food cooking, and followed her nose to the center of the settlement.

The tribe had gathered around a huge fire. For a moment doubt flooded her. This would be the second time she'd escaped. But since going back to the ash grove hadn't helped, she walked into the halo of the firelight. All of the women and some of the men gave her worried looks, but no one tried to grab her or speak to her.

"Where is Domnall?" Jenna asked one gray-haired woman with kind eyes.

"Go back, lass," the older woman said, keeping her voice low and darting looks toward a large cottage. "'Twill no' end better for you if you're found wandering." The tribeswoman sounded genuinely scared.

"I don't belong here, I know, but I've done nothing to hurt anyone. I wouldn't."

"We ken that," another, younger woman said quickly. "Only Galan—"

"How did you escape the cider house again?" a deep, hard voice demanded, silencing her.

She watched the headman stride out of the shadows. He looked angry, and the sight of him sent low murmurs through the tribe. No one challenged him, however, so Jenna decided she'd have to show them how it was done.

"The door latch was loose," she lied. "I'd like to speak with your overseer. Where is he?"

"I'm here, lass."

The big man appeared on Galan's right side, and he didn't look happy. He turned his head and let out a sharp, long whistle.

"Domnall," she said, "it's time I left." When he shook his head a little, she eyed the headman. "I didn't know you've forbidden outsiders to come here. I respect that, and I apologize for trespassing. Why don't you let me go?"

"Why indeed," Galan said, sounding

almost pleased. "Mayhap you're anxious to report to your masters."

Since she couldn't cure the headman of being an ass, she regarded Domnall. "What good does it do to keep me here?"

"Jenna, 'tis too dangerous for you to leave." People stepped out of his way as the overseer approached her. "Dangers may be waiting for you beyond the...beyond these lands. Something took the Mag Raith from our people, and marked us, and stole our memories of them, just as they did to you. If no' for the headman, we might still be trapped in the grove of stars." He saw her puzzled expression. "'Tis part of the afterlife."

He was serious, judging by the worry in his eyes. "*Galan* helped you escape the afterlife? How did he do that?"

"Hold your tongue, wench," Galan snapped.

"I don't serve you," she snapped back at him, but looked up at Domnall. "Did you ever see this grove of stars?" When he shook his head, she regarded the headman. "I wonder if you were there. Maybe it's just a story to keep you in line."

What she said sent a rush of mutters and whispers through the tribe. One short, stout man tried to quiet them, but he looked worried now, too. As for the headman, she could see the hatred in his eyes growing from heated to murderous.

Oh, yes, Jenna thought. *I believe I just blew the lid off your barrel of crap.*

"We carry the proof on our skin." Domnall touched his tattooed arm. "The Gods marked us, lass."

"Gods that you never saw, and have no memory of," Jenna reminded him. "You said that you and your men woke up in the same grove I did. You and I have matching ink. My memories are also gone. Galan had never seen me before you brought me to the settlement, so we know he didn't rescue me." She shifted her gaze to the headman. "How did you save these men from the Gods? What did they look like? How many were there? Who else was in this grove of stars? What weapons did you—"

"Silence," Galan hissed.

The druid came striding at her, and something gleamed as he pulled it out of his robe.

Before he could reach her Domnall stepped between them.

"Answer the lass," he told the headman.

"She lies," Galan shouted. He stepped back, visibly struggling for control now. "Overseer, 'tis but more evil trickery, meant to turn you against me. 'Twas why they sent the wench here."

"You still haven't answered any of my questions," Jenna said.

The short man with the worried expression stepped between them. "'Tis no harm in revealing your part in saving the Mag Raith, Headman Aedth. We'd all hear it."

Low agreements came from the rest of the Moss Dapple.

"During our harvest night I beseeched the Gods for the safe return of all souls lost." The druid's gray eyes glittered with malice. "We found the Mag Raith in the ash grove the next dawn. Thus, my entreaty must have saved you."

"Must have?" Domnall stiffened. "You didnae ken that it did?"

"What more could have brought you here?" Galan demanded. "The barrier didnae fall, yet the five of you appeared inside our boundaries. The Gods brought you to me to aid in protecting my tribe."

"Your Gods sent them, but scheming masters sent me," Jenna said, feeling grimly satisfied. "Okay. I think you're a very confused man, but either way, you weren't responsible."

Domnall whistled again, and four men came out of the shadows to flank him.

His hunters, Jenna thought, taking them in with a few surreptitious glances. The huge, dangerous-looking brute carrying a gigantic axe kept an eye on her, while the tall, lanky archer beside him held a bow ready and carried a quiver filled with arrows at his hip. At the overseer's left side stood an impossibly handsome warrior with a gleaming mane that resembled liquid onyx. He scowled at everyone as he held his sword ready. His fair-haired partner held aloft a small bird perched on his heavy leather gauntlet, and a wicked-looking dagger in his free hand.

"Mael, Edane, fetch six mounts. Broden, Kiaran, water and food for threeday. Meet us at the falls." Domnall regarded the short man. "Shaman Aklen, 'twould seem that the Mag

Raith have long repaid a debt we never owed. Six mounts seem fair payment. We'll take the lass with us, and no' return."

The shaman nodded quickly. "I wish you fair journey, Overseer."

"You'll no' be welcomed back here, Mag Raith," Galan warned. "Cross the barrier and it shall be forever closed to you and yours."

"Aye," was all Domnall said.

She didn't think leaving would be that simple, but as Domnall guided her away from the tribe no one tried to stop them. Realization of what she'd just done suddenly dawned on her: she had made Domnall and his men homeless.

"I could have handled that better," she said. "I'm sorry."

His expression remained stony. "I'm no'."

From the settlement they walked along a dark trail that led toward the sound of rushing water. As they emerged from the forest Jenna saw torches burning on either side of a dark tunnel. The passage led into the center of a waterfall that shimmered in the moonlight. It seemed very odd until she realized it wasn't making any sounds.

"'Tis an illusion," he told her. "The center of the falls isnae real."

She might have scoffed at that before she'd walked through walls. Now she found it as fascinating as everything else in this strange world.

"Is it this place that's magic, or the tribe?"

"Both." He looked past her and frowned. "Edane?"

Jenna heard a faint whistling sound, and then yelped as Domnall pushed her aside. He moved so fast she saw only a blur, and then an arrow struck the tree where she'd been standing. Its fletching bobbed from the force of the impact.

Another whizzing sound sliced through the air, but it came from behind her, and struck something in the shadows of the trail. Galan staggered out, a bow falling from his hand as he clutched the arrow piercing his palm.

The lanky redhead came to stand beside her, nocking another arrow as he kept his bow trained on the headman. "Mael comes with the horses, Overseer."

"Aye." Domnall watched without expression as Galan staggered to a tree. "We'll make for the hills once we've crossed, and find shelter for the night."

Jenna couldn't believe they were chatting so casually after what had just happened. "He was trying to kill me."

"'Tis a mistake to raise a bow against the Mag Raith, lass," Edane told her.

"Or those we protect," Kiaran said as he carried several packs out of the woods, his shoulders occupied by two of the small birds now. Three more circled down to light on his arms and head. "Sift, dinnae peck at my pate."

The bird atop his head uttered a series of short, keening sounds.

"Cease your squawking, you wee vulture," Broden said as he brought more packs and dropped them beside Kiaran's. "'Tis making *my* pate ache."

Jenna kept a wary eye on Galan, who stood with his head bowed and his hand bleeding. Then he muttered something, and the arrow impaling his palm split in half and fell to the ground. A strange energy crackled in the air between them and the headman, and all the hairs on her arms rose.

"You cannae leave, Overseer," the headman said. "You ken naught of what lay beyond our lands. Here you've my protection. In the world you shall become reviled. I'll make sure of it." He pointed at Jenna. "And this treacherous hoor shall be the cause of it."

Mael made an ugly sound and hefted his axe.

Jenna shook her head. "Next time I want to drop in on someone, please remind me to pick another forest."

"'Tis a grand one no' far from our old hunting grounds," Edane told her. "Ash a-plenty."

"No' that cursed wood," Broden said. "'Tis where treacherous, scheming evil-doers plot."

"Aye, but mayhap they'll parlay for our safe passage," Kiaran put in. "We might trade the lass for it."

"Or move back into their hideout with them," Jenna said, playing along as she looked at the headman. "Seeing as they are my tribe, it shouldn't be a problem."

Galan's face darkened so much it looked

purple now. "You dare mock me, you conniving slut."

"Secure the packs and mount up," Domnall said, and then lifted Jenna onto the smallest horse. "Ken you how to ride?"

She felt immediately at ease in the saddle, and nodded as she picked up the reins.

"'Tis no' finished between us, Mag Raith," the headman said.

Domnall swung up onto the last horse, and guided it in front of the others. "Aye, for now the debt 'tis yours."

Jenna guided her mare to follow Edane's mount, and entered the tunnel with Domnall looming behind her. Like the rest of the hunters, she didn't look back.

❧

DOMNALL STAYED close to Jenna during the passage through the falls and then down the center of what appeared as a raging river. She flinched when her mare entered the second illusion, and then gaped as the furious waters receded.

"That's a very neat trick," she told him,

glancing down at the dry ground beneath her mount's hooves. "I'll have to show you mine once we get to wherever we're going. Where are we going?"

He nodded toward the northern hills. "We'll take shelter and rest there for the night, and speak more on the matter."

"Shall we too sing songs by the fire?" Broden asked, his harsh voice stinging with bitterness. "Or better to beseech the Gods to deliver a soul to Galan, for he's none of his own."

Knowing the trapper to be the voice of all the hunters' discontent, Domnall said, "If we'd ended him, Brother, he'd only come back."

"Aye, but I'd have enjoyed it." Broden glanced at Jenna. "What say you, wench? 'Twould gladden you to see the *dru-wid* dead, or to mewl at me for forgiveness?"

"You forget, I'm a treacherous hoor," she replied, her expression calm. "I'd help you kill him."

All the other men laughed, and even Domnall chuckled. Broden gave her a narrow look before he rode ahead to flank Mael.

The ride into the hills took some hours, slowed by the darkness and a cold, damp night wind. By the time they reached a spot by a stream suitable to make camp Jenna sat low in the saddle, her shoulders drooping. Domnall resisted the urge to pluck her from the mare and hold her against him, as he had in the cottage. This would be the first of many such jaunts, and openly coddling the lass would only spark new resentment among his hunters.

As Mael and Edane tended to their mounts, Domnall sent Kiaran and Broden to collect stones and firewood. He turned to check on Jenna, and saw her taking bread and fruit from the packs and arranging it for a meal on a clean blanket.

"Here, lass." He offered her a water skin. "You must be parched."

"Thanks." She took a swallow and then met his gaze. "Don't worry, I'm fine. It's just been a long day."

Again she showed *tapachd* as if she were one of his hunters. "For us all, lass."

Domnall sorted through the packs until he found a firesteel, and gathered some dry grasses to bundle into kindling. When his archer and falconer returned with the makings for a camp fire, he helped them build it and sparked the flames, nursing them with his breath until they enveloped the dried wood.

The warmth drew them all closer as they ate and drank, and Jenna sighed with tired pleasure as she held her slim hands close to the blaze. "This is nice."

"Your hands show you've done fine work," Kiaran said. "What does an architect, then?"

"We draw designs for buildings." She made a face. "Only I don't remember anything I've done."

"Yet you ken that as your work." The falconer gestured to the ground. "Will you draw now such a place?"

Jenna picked up a twig, closed her eyes for a moment, and then began to etch lines into the dirt. The sure, rapid movements of her hand made it apparent that she felt at ease with the task. When she finished Domnall eyed the shapes and small symbols she had drawn, unable to fathom what they represented.

Kiaran leaned over to examine it. "I dinnae ken what 'tis."

"It's called a *parti*, a preliminary sketch for a building," Jenna said. "Each shape I've drawn represents a space inside the construct, and every symbol an important feature for moving through it." She pointed to a slash inside the largest box. "This diagonal line here is the entry, for example, and the arc shows how the door opens."

"From above, then." The falconer cocked his head. "'Tis as what a bird sees."

"That's exactly right," she said, smiling.

Now that he knew how to look at it, Domnall finally recognized what she had drawn. "'Tis the cider house." A crack of lightning made him glance up to see a storm gathering. "We'll need to find shelter."

Mael stood, his own gazed fixed on the clouds, which had begun flashing from within with huge bursts of light. "'Tis something above there."

A thin jag of bright white came down to strike a tree not a stone's throw away from their camp. The air filled with the crackling fury of the impact as bark shattered and blasted outward. Mael cursed and jumped out of the way as the trunk split and half the tree fell toward him. The ruined wood landed with a crash, shaking the ground.

Jenna's head tilted back, and she made a strangled sound.

"'Tis but a storm, lass," Edane told her. "'Twill pass."

Domnall followed the direction of her gaze and what he saw made him draw his sword. "By the Gods."

Dozens of creatures, unlike any he'd ever seen, emerged and descended from the clouds. Each glowed with thunderous light as they glided on enormous, glittering wings. As they came down, a strange, growing hum spread through the air. They flew like birds but appeared to be god-like men in their forms and faces. The garments they wore seemed made of wide ribbons, and fluttered around their magnificent bodies as streamers would. Each stared down at one of the hunters, but the largest and brightest flew straight for Jenna.

"Sluath," she said, her face gone completely white.

The word she uttered made something tighten in Domnall's chest and rumble through his limbs, sending sizzling heat along his inked arm. Every Pritani knew the legends of the Sluath, the soul-devouring demons who rode the storms in search of mortals made helpless.

"Get the mounts," he shouted over the growing din.

He seized the lass and carried her off to the shelter of the nearest tree. Lightning struck it a moment later, pelting them with a shower of exploding wood as the Sluath plunged down, their claw-tipped hands extended.

Jenna made a low sound and dropped like a stone.

Domnall caught her and flung her over his shoulder, but had no time to avoid the descending demons. Mael rode in just as one creature tried to snatch Jenna from Domnall's grip. As the tracker collided with the glowing demon, light burst out, enveloping the tracker. Mael and his stallion grew as bright as the Sluath, and left the ground to ride up into the air.

Domnall stared in disbelief as man and horse took flight. But with each full stretch of the beast's galloping legs, the pair rose higher. For a moment Mael clung to the horse's mane as he stared down at the ground falling away below him. But in the next instant, the tracker spurred his heel's into his horse's flanks. As they rose even higher, he let loose a savage and bellowing whoop.

Edane rode in fast, leading Domnall's horse beside him. He jumped up into the saddle, and light enveloped him, the lass, and the horse. A moment later he rose high into the air with Mael and the other hunters. To his surprise they rode as surely and easily as if they still remained on the ground.

"We facking fly," Broden shouted, as he galloped past him.

One of the creatures came at Domnall, its black wings and streaming garments making its skull face glow ghastly white. The shock of nearly colliding with the skeletal apparition nearly unseated him, but it also helped him avoid the bolt of lightning that arced between them. The massive jag of light glanced off Kiaran's tack, who clung to his horse's neck as his saddle split in half.

"She's mine," a cold voice said from

above, and the white-winged Sluath made another soaring dive for Jenna.

Domnall jerked the lass down to shield her with his body, and wheeled his mount around. The creature slammed into his back. He felt his tunic tear, and the bright pain of the Sluath's claws scoring deep trenches into his flesh. Then Broden crashed into it, knocking it away before he rode off in heated pursuit of another air demon.

The battle continued until the clouds suddenly lifted, taking the Sluath with them. A moment later they had vanished, and the Mag Raith slowly circled down until their mounts once more stood on solid earth. All of the hunters bore ugly wounds from fighting the creatures, and Domnall could feel the blood dripping down his back.

Edane dismounted, tottering a little before he reached Domnall and Jenna. He lifted his bloodied arms. "To me."

Domnall handed Jenna down to his archer before he got off his horse and jerked off the shreds of his tunic. As the furious wind whipped around him, he felt the raw gashes across his back shrinking as they healed.

"By all the Gods," Broden said breathlessly, reining in his mount. Despite the gashes about his shoulders, his face was flushed with excitement. "We flew with the very storm."

Mael joined them, clapping Broden on the back. The tracker's cheek bore an ugly bruise but his eyes shone bright—until he saw Jenna in Edane's arms.

"The lass?" he said, as Broden followed his gaze and sobered as well.

"Fainted away," Edane said looking down into her face.

Domnall looked at his battered men. "We find cover and make ready for a stand hunt. Gather the packs."

Chapter Seven

Riding the last of the storm's currents, Prince Iolar led the Sluath to ground, alighting in a shadowy glen cloaked in mist. As soon as their boots touched the soil their wings retracted, folding to hide beneath their flowing garments. He invoked the glamor they used while beyond the underworld, transforming himself and his *deamhanan* with the guise of ordinary humans.

Without looking at his surroundings, he could sense that there was no underworld portal near. The tedium of having to walk the mortal realm, until another storm came that they could ride, settled upon him like a smothering cloak. As creatures of the air the Sluath belonged in the sky, not tramping about in the dirt.

He sniffed the air, catching a trace of human, but it came from the direction opposite that of the highlanders.

"My lord," Danar said. The largest of his scouts came to him bearing blades in both fists. "It seems the rebels survived their escape."

"My eyes still work," Iolar informed him. The prince had been more interested in recovering the woman, who would have provided him with much-needed distraction and sport. "Puzzling that they ascended on their nags to fight us. Not a reunion I expected."

"They're stronger and faster now," Clamhan said. He was still shrouded in black and wearing the skull mask he used to terrify mortals. "Perhaps they begin to alter."

Iolar sighed. "If they'd done that, they'd have welcomed our arrival and handed me my due. Did anyone see my treasure?" His *deamhanan* all remained silent. "How disappointing." He glanced over at the smallest of their legion, a cunning *deamhan* who appeared as a young lad bedecked in blooms.

"Meirneal, what of your pet brute? I saw him among the others. You claimed you'd brought that lout to heel."

The diminutive Sluath bared small, sharp teeth. "It would seem that he's abandoned his devotion to me, my lord."

"Grant us leave to pursue the rebels, my prince." Even glamor could not contain Seabhag's inconstant form which, in his agitation, shifted from toothy monster to winsome maiden. "For soon they'll crawl back to wherever they've hid these past centuries, and we'll lose them."

The scent of human grew strong, and Iolar saw some of the other *deamhanan* turn toward it. Denied the pleasures promised by the dark-haired woman, his own hunger increased.

"Fresh prey draws nearer," Iolar said. "Cloak yourselves."

The Sluath disappeared into the mist while Iolar prepared to drop his glamor. As soon as the male came into view, however, he saw his peculiar garments and uttered a vile curse. The only humans the Sluath could not enslave were the tree-worshippers. The wretched beings, called druids by other humans, could be trapped and tormented but not culled. While mortal they had inviolate souls. Still, the druid might provide some brief amusement when Iolar tore him from his mount and yanked his limbs from their sockets.

A short distance from the glen the tree-worshipper dismounted and tethered his horse before striding with purpose toward Iolar.

"You, there," the druid said, his face dark with ire. "I seek five highlanders accompanied by a black-haired hoor. Did they pass you?"

Iolar frowned as he took in the tree-worshipper's unusual stature. The male stood nearly as tall as Danar, and had the muscular form of a warrior. He also radiated power that held more than a tinge of darkness to it. His despair, which carried like the rankness of rot, possessed the heat of rage rather than the chill of sorrow.

"Dinnae stand there gaping at me," the druid said, his tone sharp now. "Did you see them?"

Dropping his glamor, Iolar spread his wings. "See me, human, from your knees."

The druid swayed, squinting against the brilliant light shed by the prince's true form, yet remained standing. *"You're Sluath."*

"Allow me to kiss it, my lord," Meirneal said, a lovely smile spreading across his young face as the others uncloaked as well. "I'll persuade it to obey."

Clamhan uttered a laugh. "You'll chew off the tongue again, and then it will tell us nothing."

Iolar walked up to the druid and seized him by the throat, lifting him off his feet.

"I am Iolar, Prince of all Sluath." He waited for the druid to struggle and choke, and when he didn't, he smiled. "Are you insane or simply a very bad druid?"

"Release me." He choked out the words, but never took his gray eyes from the prince's face. "Or I shall gut you."

Iolar glanced down to see the tree-worshipper's fist pressing a blade against his chest plate. The novelty of being threatened by a human—even one as close to damnation as this one had crept—made him laugh before he dropped him.

"I'm Galan Aedth," the druid said,

rubbing his neck before he sheathed his blade. "Headman of the Moss Dapple tribe."

He said it with great self-importance, as if it made them equals. The gall of this pitiful being seemed to have no limits.

"I don't care what you call yourself, human," Iolar declared. "But the five highlanders and their hoor. Tell me of them."

Galan's eyes shifted left and right as if seeing the *deamhanan* for the first time. But instead of fear, a sly look slid into place.

"So we both seek the Pritani hunters," the druid said as his gaze moved past him to the road leading around the glen. "Mayhap we could aid each other."

A druid who bargained with a *deamhan* prince that he'd just threatened might be worth tolerating for a few more seconds.

"Please," Iolar said pleasantly, "do enlighten me."

"Before that hoor lured them away, the Mag Raith served me."

Iolar exchanged a look with Seabhag, who raised his brows. So the highlanders had hid with druids.

Galan gestured at the prince's blood-stained claws. "I neednae use force to prevail over them. I ken all their skills."

Iolar suspected that was all the explanation he'd offer. The druid's deviousness didn't surprise him, as he knew the trait to be common among that kind. Still, he could prove useful, especially now that he'd revealed his utter ignorance of the Sluath's natures. Yes, while they searched from the air, the druid could plod along on the ground.

"What do you want in return for your, ah, services?"

"My mate wasnae druid kind, but Pritani. She died in childbirth." Old suffering burned in his eyes. "If you've the power to bring her back to me, I shall do anything you wish."

That seemed to be the only whole truth that had issued from the druid's endlessly flapping lips. Despite his contempt for the human, Iolar was somewhat intrigued.

"Your hunters stole from me before they escaped the underworld. If you wish your mate restored to you, then you must first find them and lead them to me. Only then shall I resurrect your mate."

Galan sank to his knees. "I give you my vow, my prince."

In that moment he felt the rush of greed pouring out of the druid, and smiled. "Very well, then, Aedth. I think we may have a bargain."

Chapter Eight

Never had Broden felt more alive than when he and his mount had taken to the air. To ride across the sky, as if they'd both sprouted feathers and wings, had broken all the unseen chains binding his spirit. The utter exhilaration of it had poured such raw power through him he'd expected his body might burst apart in the way that a dropped pot shattered. He craved it again, to give chase and hunt down those hoor-faced *skegs*. This time they'd taste his blade with their pretty necks before their pretty heads plummeted to thump in the dirt.

Yet Domnall had issued the order for a stand hunt. That meant they would need to find a concealed place to provide cover, and that duty fell to Broden. Flying to hunt the demons would have to wait.

Pushing back a surge of resentment, Broden took in their surroundings, turning slowly as he inspected every possible route away from the battlefield. The passage of time had altered the look of the highlands both subtly and greatly. Beneath that changed surface he knew the rocky terrain to be as it ever had been: a warren of stone.

The *skeg* bastarts would expect them to flee, so no place could be safer than exactly where they had fought them.

Broden shifted his gaze to the slopes, noting the patterns of weathered stone and brush growth. There between two rough outcroppings he saw a patch of promising darkness.

He regarded the overseer. "We stay, and climb." He pointed at what he'd spotted. "'Twill be a cave there."

"See if 'tis suitable," Domnall said, and glanced at the unconscious lass in Edane's arms. "Quickly."

Broden left his mount behind with the others as he ascended to scout the site. The incline proved wide and level enough for the horses, and the entry to the cave passable. Before stepping inside, he tossed in a rock and then listened to its clatter. Nothing came out, but the echo suggested a chamber large enough to hide them all. He started to turn, and then looked down to see the overseer hovering beside the archer, both of them studying the lass's still features.

Domnall willnae take her in without certainty.

After making a quick torch from a pine cone impaled on a green branch, Broden lit the end and entered the cave. He moved the flame from side to side, inspecting the rubble-strewn floor, glistening walls and toothy ceiling. Water dripped from an unseen crevice into a rain pool off to the side. A breach in the back wall made it plain that a second chamber lay beyond the first.

"Flee or die," he called out, and the wretched rasp of his own voice mocked him twice more.

Then another did, twisting his words: *From this ye cannae flee.*

Broden turned around, but the softly malicious voice had come from within his head.

They had been the final words his sire's mate, Sileas, had spoken to him. She had come the night before he'd gone on his last hunt to tell him that his sire had been killed in battle. Thanks to her, his tribe finally had found a use for Broden.

The Carac shall make war upon us unless we appease their headman and his particular desire for strong, handsome lads. She walked around him like a stockman inspecting a young bull, prodding him here and there to test the bulk of his muscle. *Aye, ye shall well please him. Strong as an ox, alluring as a prince. I reckon he'll use ye nightly.*

Unable to fathom such a fate, Broden stared at her. *Ye cannae do this. I'm the headman's son.*

I *birthed his son.* Her hand slammed into his cheek with a loud crack. *Ye're my slave, now of some worth. Dinnae reckon the Mag Raith shall offer ye protection. From this ye cannae flee.*

The torch's flame began to sputter as the cone glowed orange-red to its core. Broden strode back to the gap and looked through it to see another, larger cave that would hold a dozen horses with ease. It, too, stood empty, like everything inside Broden since Sileas had declared him a slave, and the vow he'd made himself after she'd left him.

Broden had gone on that hunt to have one last day with his friends. When they returned, he had planned to pack his few belongings and leave the Mag Raith, just as Sileas had ordered. She believed she'd stolen his freedom, and sent him to a wretched fate, but in truth she had made him an instrument of his own vengeance.

Broden had never returned from the hunt, so what he would have done had never come to pass.

Sileas, the tribes, and most of the trapper's hatred of them had long since rotted away. Now and then Broden would wake in the night, awash in sweat and trembling with fear. He never knew what caused his terror, but he always reached for a dagger, feeling such self-loathing that death seemed a mercy. Yet each time the blade had fallen unused from his grasp. For that he blamed Domnall and the others, who gave him reason and purpose, and brotherhood he would never have otherwise known.

The torch flared a final time before it died,

leaving the trapper standing alone in a black void.

'Tis what Jenna feels.

Though she'd said little, Broden recognized something of himself in her. It was as if she, too, had once faced the unimaginable, and nothing since could unsettle her. He also wondered if she ever reached for a dagger in the night.

He glanced over at the faint glimmer from the front cave. As he had every day since awaking in the ash grove, Broden turned away from the darkness and went toward the light.

Chapter Nine

J enna woke to the coppery taste of blood in her mouth, and feeling as if she'd swallowed a bucket of sand. She lay flat on her back inside a shadowy place. A dull headache hammered at her temples with a slow, painful beat. She'd also bitten the inside of her cheek, judging by how sore it felt.

"Sip a wee bit, lass," Edane said as he appeared above her, and held the edge of a wooden cup to her mouth. "You've had a fearsome time of it."

She took a swallow of the water, which eased the dryness in her throat, and looked at the dark space around them. Some reed-thin stems thrust into a cracked boulder a few feet

away burned like candles. Their scant light
made the rough stone walls sparkle here and
there. Above her she saw the tips of what
resembled dull gray icicles.

They'd taken refuge inside a cave.

Thanks to the lights she could just make
out the silhouettes of the other hunters, who
stood several yards away. Two of the men held
a wall of leafy branches on either side while
Domnall stuffed handfuls of grass or moss into
its gaps. Mael stood peering through one hole,
watching for something.

"'Tis a blind they build," the archer told
her. "'Twill prevent those bastarts from seeing
us while we keep watch for them."

Recalling how the glowing, winged creatures had spiraled down from the sky made
her shudder. As beautiful as they'd looked,
everything about them had made her skin feel
too tight and her heart thunder. She swallowed some bile.

"They're Sluath," she said.

Edane coaxed her into taking another
drink before he set aside the cup, not meeting
her gaze.

She pushed herself upright. "Don't you believe me?"

"My tribe warned of such demons to keep the younglings from roaming at night," the archer admitted. "Mayhap yours spun the same tales."

"I can't be Pritani. If I were, then I'd talk like you and the others. I don't. I'm not from here. I'm not a druid." Saying the last word made her feel even more confident in her claims. She didn't even pronounce it the way the Mag Raith did. "The Sluath are not scary stories. They're real."

Edane frowned. "You remember the winged demons from your past?"

"I've seen them before tonight." Of that much she was sure. She rose to her feet. "Domnall recognized them too."

As she tottered a little Edane braced her with a hand on her back. "Turn your back to the light, lass."

She did as he asked, and felt air coming through holes in the back of the borrowed tunic. He went and took one of the reed lights from the rock.

"What's happened?" she asked.

"One of the creatures clawed Domnall's back," Edane said as he held the flaming reed closer. "You've tears in the tunic as if 'twas done to you the same, but I cannae see wounds."

"It probably happened when I fell." Though Edane looked as if he were going to ask her a question, thinking of the Sluath touching her made her feel nauseated and shaky. "I need to do something before I throw up."

He hesitated a moment but nodded toward the back of the cave. "We should see to the horses."

Jenna followed him into a larger chamber lit by a single torch. All six mounts stood where they had been hobbled, and still wore their saddles.

"Leave on the bridles," the archer told her as he went to the biggest horse. "We may ride without saddles, but we'll want the reins."

Jenna watched how Edane unstrapped and removed the saddle before she did the same for the mare she'd ridden. The horse felt cold, and she found bits of frost clinging to her hide in various spots.

The shining Sluath that had come at her had done that. She'd felt the stinging scratch of the snowflakes on her face just before she'd passed out. How could a thing that looked so mesmerizing and lovely make her tremble with so much fear and rage, when nothing else in this place had?

Edane gave her a cloth to use to rub down the mare. "We cannae graze them until the morrow, but…" He pointed to a depression in the stone floor that ran long and deep enough for all six horses. "We can manage a trough."

"Do we have enough water for them?"

The archer nodded. "'Tis a rain pool in the front chamber with fresh water."

She and Edane spent the next half-hour filling waterskins there and emptying them into the makeshift trough. By the time they finished, the other hunters had the blind completed.

"Eat and rest. I'll stand the rise watch," Domnall told the men before he regarded Jenna. "You've recovered?"

He sounded polite, as if they were strangers, but he watched her face with such intensity that it all but announced she was the only thing in the world that mattered. She decided that she wouldn't give him more to worry about.

"My head hurts, and my shirt's torn, but otherwise I'm all right." As he gestured to her, she followed him over to the blind. She looked out through the only gap left in the branches to scan outside. "Can the Sluath find us here?"

"They wouldnae reckon to look where they left us, and Mael scattered our tracks." He glanced at her for a moment, as if unsure of what to say. "You named these creatures. What more do you ken of them?"

"They're evil." She wrapped her arms around her waist. "And that one that glowed white and gold, the way he was staring and smiling at me, he knew me. He wanted me, and I couldn't..." She pulled in her bottom lip until the sob that threatened to come out went away. "I thought I'd die if he touched me."

"Aye. I saw your terror." Domnall touched her shoulder, his fingertips moving in a subtle, reassuring caress. "He'll no' have you again."

Which meant he suspected, just as she did, that the Sluath had gotten her before tonight.

"Do you remember your tribe's stories about them?"

"My sire didnae indulge in such, but others spoke of them by the night fires." His hand slipped down over her arm before he drew it away. "'Twas said the Sluath once lived as men do, but their wickedness blackened and then shriveled their souls. When their lives ended, they became cursed nomads, ever wandering the land seeking mortals left lost or hurt and alone. Those never missed 'twere their favorite prey. They'd steal them and enslave them for eternity."

"In the underworld?" Jenna asked.

He moved his shoulders. "'Twas told to me that they dwelled in storms. Travelers never went out in the night unless 'twas clear skies, for fear the Sluath would fall upon them."

Jenna took in a quick breath. "Like they did to us tonight."

The overseer shook his head. "'Twas but a story, lass. If the Sluath had taken you, you'd no' be here."

"Or they did, and I escaped," she countered, and then made the next leap. "Like you and your men."

Chapter Ten

✦❧✦

As Domnall watched the moon rise, he welcomed the deep stillness of the night. Much had happened in a short time. They had escaped Galan's yoke of lies only to find that the truth might yet be worse. His hand tightened on the pommel of his sword. They had escaped the Sluath.

Even without seeing him and his men rise into the sky to do battle with the vile creatures, the lass had conjured up the notion. In his bones, Domnall felt the rightness of it. He thanked the comradeship of centuries that had kept his brothers from speaking of the battle in front of her. He knew that they, like him, would want to mull over every strange detail—but not in front of the lass for fear of revealing much else.

Domnall gazed up at the milky face of the moon. He already knew that the answers to his men's unspoken questions wouldn't come from talk. There was only one place where they might finally get to the truth.

As the moon reached its peak, Mael came to stand watch. He spoke softly to avoid disturbing the others.

"I'll wake you at dawn," the tracker said. He nodded at the slumbering forms of the other hunters, and the one person still sitting up and watching the last of the rush lights burn low. "She's no' ate nor slept, poor lass. She'll no' ask for solace but 'tis what she's sore needing."

Domnall nodded and retreated into the cave, where he drank some water and collected a pear and some bread. Treading silently to where Jenna sat, he eased down beside her.

"Share food with me," he murmured as he drew his dagger. When she didn't reply he cut a portion of the fruit and held it in front of her mouth. "Eat, or I'll wake Broden to hand-feed you."

Jenna took a quick bite, but she didn't chew as if hungered.

"'Tis safe now, lass." It had grown too dark to see what lingered in her eyes, but he felt her worry as if she wore a cloak woven of it. "They'll no' find us here."

He heard her swallow. "There is no us. I'm not one of you. I'll go on from here by myself."

Whatever doubts about Jenna still lingered in Domnall's mind, her offer crushed them to dust. Few hardened Pritani warriors would possess such *tapachd*.

"You could," he agreed, cutting another slice for her. "You may reach a village or farm in twoday or three. Aye, if the sky remains clear, and those creatures dinnae track you. If no rogues or thieves find you alone and defenseless. If you dinnae fall into a loch or over a cliff or down a slope. Have you a map, and a destination in mind?"

She pushed away the second piece of fruit he offered. "I'm not helpless."

"You've much courage, I'll grant you, but

you're far from your home. You've no memory of yourself or your kin. You ken naught of Scotland. You'd be alone." He set aside the food and took hold of her cold hand. The instant he did, he felt the ink on his arm grow warm. "Dinnae blame yourself for the attack, Jenna. You didnae summon the Sluath."

"But they knew me." She met his gaze just before the last of the rush lights sputtered out. "They'll keep looking for me. I can feel it."

So could he, and he hated it. "They'll no' take you."

"You've already lost your home because of me. I can't let you and the others lose every-thing." Her shoulders rounded, and she ducked her head. "I'm not worth your lives."

Telling her the truth of that might only compound her fears. Now Domnall wondered if he should wake Edane. The archer ever proved far better than he at managing females, and seemed to understand the lass. But as soon as that thought entered his head, he discarded it. He'd found Jenna, he'd taken her away from the tribe, and now he'd help her through this.

Stretching out beside her, he tugged her

down until she lay on her side. "On the morrow, we must ride the day through," he told her. "I'll keep you safe, lass. Now close your eyes."

She made a small, disgruntled sound. "Does anyone ever say no to you?"

"Galan, and you." He felt her shake with a suppressed chuckle, and smiled. "Put your head on my shoulder. Aye, 'tis the way."

Jenna remained stiff for a moment, and then finally shifted closer to him. "You said that you and your men were hunters before you landed in the ash grove."

Domnall eased his arm around her. "Aye."

"Why don't you ever..." She interrupted herself with a yawn. "...hunt anything?"

So, she'd noticed that much. "We've food enough. When we dinnae, we'll hunt."

Domnall remained awake until he felt her gradually go limp and heard her breathing slow. He'd shared his bed countless times with a willing *dru-widess*, but they'd never lingered after the facking had ended. Now he would sleep with a female he'd seen naked and wanted more than any he'd ever known, but had not taken. It bemused him, more so than even finding her in the grove.

Jenna turned to him, her slender arm sliding across his waist. For such a wee lass she generated enough heat to warm him, and the scent of her skin colored every breath he took. This was why the *dru-widesses* never remained the night. In some ways sleeping together seemed even more intimate than sharing pleasures.

At his post Mael remained alert and watchful, so Domnall at last closed his eyes. He drifted into the only sleep he'd permit himself, a light doze that any sudden sound would end. His thoughts reshaped the darkness into the glen where they had meant to make camp for the night. There he watched his men go about their tasks, and saw Jenna once more putting out food for their meal. This time he didn't take his gaze from her as the clouds gathered overhead. He saw her expression after the first shaft of lightning struck, but it was not fearful.

She looked furious.

The choked sound she made came from rage as well. She moved her hand to her side, reaching for something when nothing was there. But Domnall knew exactly what she meant to grasp: a blade.

Light streaked down from the Sluath, moving over Jenna's taut features. The light, not fear, had made her look so pale. When she next said the only word to pass her lips, she spat it like a curse.

Sluath.

Domnall had no doubt at all now that Jenna knew the Sluath, and hated them with all her being. He'd never seen such pure loathing on a female's face. It matched the fury that rose inside him, then and now, even in the dream.

She's mine, the Sluath had said.

No, Domnall thought, smashing his fist through the illusion. *I'd first end her myself.*

The savagery of his dream jolted him awake. Thin gray light filtered through the blind with the arrival of dawn. He looked down to see Jenna watching him.

"If they take us, and we can't escape," she murmured, as if she could see every thought in his head, "I want you to kill me. I don't

know if I can... Just promise me that
you will."

Domnall had never harmed a single lass in
his long life. He couldn't imagine what would
cause him to do so. Females had to be cher-
ished and protected. But somehow, she knew
that death would be better than being taken
by the Sluath. In his heart, so did he.

His hand felt heavy as he reached down
and tugged his smallest dirk from his boot.
The light, thin blade had a finely-honed edge
and a point that would part flesh as if it
were water.

"You're certain?" he asked as he pressed
the hilt into her hand. She nodded. "You've
my word, then."

Jenna's bottom lip trembled, and she slung
her arm across his chest as if to embrace him.
But instead she quickly rolled over and got to
her feet, tucking the dirk in the side of
her boot.

Domnall put the horrific agreement out of
his mind as he went to join Mael. "Any sign?"

The tracker shook his head. "We should
graze the mounts while we break our fast."

Leading the horses out of the caves and

down the incline with Mael, they found a patch of lush grasses and hobbled them there. Kiaran came to keep watch and let his birds hunt for their morning meal, while the other hunters carried out their packs. Jenna emerged last, carrying their refilled waterskins slung over both narrow shoulders.

Domnall told Kiaran of his intent and the falconer nodded his consent. When they joined the others Broden handed out oatcakes baked with nuts and berries while Edane sliced a wedge of cheese to top them. No one spoke as they ate, but Jenna, he noted, kept as watchful an eye on the horizon as Mael.

"We cannae remain in these hills," Domnall finally said. "We'll go west, to the highlands where we last hunted. The fortress where we sheltered that night may yet stand."

"After so long, Overseer?" Edane said, his brows knitted together. "Surely there couldnae be any trace left of us at Dun Chaill."

"Why?" Jenna asked, looking from Edane to Domnall. "How long has it been since you went there?"

"We didnae count the days," Broden said

quickly before Domnall could answer. "What matters the time passed?"

Jenna shrugged. "I was just curious." She brushed some crumbs from her trews and stood. "I'll go help Kiaran with the horses."

Once she'd walked away Broden leaned forward. "The lass is a worn bow string, near to snapping. Dinnae set another nock to her."

The trapper's rough compassion didn't surprise him as much as his perception of Jenna's fragile emotions.

"Aye," Domnall said. "'Twill keep."

Chapter Eleven

Over the next day Jenna paid in full for the scanty amount of sleep she'd gotten in the cave. The hunters rode at a quick, steady lope out of the hills and into a wide valley, stopping only to rest the horses a few times. She managed to keep up, but only just. Somehow, she knew to relax as much as she could, moving her body with the mare to minimize the impact of the jolting gait. From the way her muscles were knotting, however, it seemed obvious that she hadn't been on horseback in a while.

At midday they reached a river crossing the valley. Domnall held up his fist, and all the hunters slowed and then dismounted. Jenna did the same, wincing as her back and bottom gave her a preview of the considerable pain she could expect tonight. She led the mare to drink at the river's edge, and then took a good look around at the forests marching up the high slopes on either side of them. Snow whitened the rounded tops of the mountains, but everything else was green and dotted with wildflowers. The air smelled like a dewy garden that had gone wild.

"'Tis wider now," she heard Edane say to Kiaran, who walked back and forth along the bank with him. "By half again as much."

"What's wider?" she asked the archer, who started to gesture toward the water and then dropped his hand.

"An old trail we passed," he said. "Come, you should walk with me, lass. 'Twill keep your legs from stiffening."

And prevent me from asking more questions.

All day she had ended murmured conversations with just a glance. Normally men of few words, the hunters had become positively tight-lipped. No matter how much they said to her, she sensed an iceberg of what hadn't been said beneath the surface.

She accompanied Edane down river,

where they stopped to admire a series of short, cascading falls.

"You don't have to lie to me, Edane. Just tell me to mind my own business."

"I dinnae ken business." His gaze shifted past her, and then he grinned like a boy. "Gods blind me. 'Tis the pass over there, I'm sure of it. By your leave, lass."

Jenna watched him trot back to the other hunters, where he pointed at a break in the ridges on the north side of the valley. It appeared closer than it probably was, and they'd have to keep riding their tired horses at a fast pace to reach it before sunset. As exhausted and stiff as she felt, she wondered if she should ask Domnall to tie her onto the mare.

You've been through so much worse.

She remembered saying that, but not to who or why or when. Her voice just echoed in a void, as if she'd been talking to herself. She wandered back toward the hunters, and sat down on a flat-topped rock. When Mael brought her a waterskin and what looked like a small bun, she smiled her thanks. Biting into the bread, she got a mouthful of a jellied filling that tasted of honey and spices.

"*Oh*." The delicious shock of it made her eyelashes flutter. "Please tell me you have more of these."

"A bag full, aye." He hefted a small sack. "'Tis made by the *dru-widesses* for their ritual nights. I reckoned they could make more when they found them gone."

The tracker also gave her a piece of smoked fish and a thin wooden cup filled with a cold, minty brew before he sat down at the base of the rock to enjoy his own share. Jenna felt better as soon as she finished the meal, and when she went to wash her sticky fingers in the river her muscles hardly protested.

"You've done well," Domnall said as he crouched beside her. "I'd stay another hour to give you more rest, but if we're to reach the fortress by nightfall we cannae linger."

"I know." She looked up at the thin white clouds trailing across the sky before she regarded him. "We'll have to take cover if there's another storm."

He nodded. "Mael shall keep watch for sheltering we can use along the path. Once we ride through the pass, we'll be but a league from Dun Chaill."

She had no idea how far a league was but hoped it was roughly equivalent to a mile.

"What is Dun Chaill?"

"'Tis what the Pritani called the fortress where we sheltered before we became lost."

"Does Galan know about this place?" When he shook his head, she felt surprised. "Why didn't you tell him about it?"

His jaw tightened. "We never speak of that night."

Domnall obviously didn't want her to ask anything more about it, either. Demanding to know why they were all worried about talking openly in front of her wouldn't help matters.

"I'm ready when you are."

The hours that followed their brief stop proved just as brutal as the morning ride, but Jenna kept pace with the men. The sun had started its final drop toward the horizon as they left the valley and guided the horses into the narrow, rocky pass. There the shadows of the surrounding mountains and the winds pouring through the gap dropped the temperature from pleasant to chilly. Jenna had to

clench her teeth to keep them from chattering
as they slowed their mounts to a careful walk.

A body-warmed cloak suddenly swaddled
her, and she glanced over at Kiaran, who now
just had a thin tunic covering his chest.

"You'll regret this," Jenna warned him.

"I've friends to keep me warm," he said as
two kestrels landed on his shoulders. "And you
willnae look so bonny with blue lips."

Broden rode between them. "Keep up," he
said before he guided his horse in front
of hers.

His new position blocked most of the
wind, she discovered, and with the warmth of
Kiaran's cloak her chill quickly dispersed.

The last of the sunlight vanished as they
emerged from the pass, riding into a broad,
thick forest that looked even older than the
Moss Dapple's lands. All of the trees around
them had grown to enormous sizes, and had
the tough, weathered look of enduring countless seasons of sunshine and snow. The moss
clinging to their trunks spread down to the
forest floor, forming a thick, uninterrupted
carpet of mottled green. She didn't spot a
single trail, which suggested that no one had

been in these woods for years, maybe even decades.

An odd relief warmed Jenna as she looked up at the clear sky overhead, glittering with countless stars. She didn't recognize anything, but the forest felt like home. Could she have come from a place like this? Maybe her people lived near here, or occupied a territory very similar to it.

The hunters all stopped in the middle of the woods. Domnall also reined in his mount and jumped down, striding forward toward a cluster of trees. He reached between them, and then glanced back.

"'Tis here," he called.

"'Tis grown much," Mael said, looking around them. Unlike her he seemed worried now.

Kiaran's birds glided off to a nearby tree as he swung down and then helped Jenna dismount. "Stay with Mael," he told her before he went to join the overseer, and they both disappeared into the trees.

As she walked up to where the tracker stood her gaze caught the first of several unnatural lines running through the woods.

Moonlight illuminated a rounded wall encir-
cling a huge oak, and a lower pile of collapsed
stones rough with crumbling layers of mortar.
Another, more intact wall angled away from it,
interrupted by a rectangular void that must
have once been a gate or door.

Following the ruins and filling in the lines
of the missing structures, Jenna picked out the
shape of a partially-collapsed tower, and two
more beyond it. The trees hid a great deal of
the outer structure, but her architect's brain
still knew what it was looking at.

"It's a castle," she murmured, and caught
Mael's surprised glance. "Or it was a castle, a
long time ago."

"'Twas but a small fortress when last we
came here," he said, and surveyed the exposed
structures. "I dinnae recall the place as large
as 'tis now."

Edane brought some branches he'd gathered, and with Mael's help fashioned them
into torches. He handed one to Jenna. "Best
stay here while we've a look, lass."

"So the Sluath can swoop down and grab
me while you're gone?" She shook her head.
"I'm coming with you."

Chapter Twelve

Drenched in sweat and yet feeling as if he'd been embraced by the Gods themselves, Galan rode back to the settlement. He had to stop several times along the way to rest, but he attributed the weakness he felt to the shock of the encounter with the Sluath.

The legends had not been outlandish tales. The demons were real. The fact that they pursued the Mag Raith said much of how the hunters might have resurrected and acquired their special gifts.

And how I shall acquire mine.

Once he reached the river, he dismounted and led his horse through the water illusions and into the tunnel passage through the falls.

Aside from the exhaustion, he felt as he had in his first incarnation. In that life he had grown powerful and respected, a spell-caster of such promise the tribe had whispered of his being summoned to join the conclave. This night that old sense of coming glory returned to him.

He had challenged the most astonishing creatures in existence, the very stuff of legends, and had brought them under his sway.

Before this night the Sluath had only ever been ridiculous tales uttered by scolding mothers and superstitious elders. Now with his own eyes he had looked upon the cold, beautiful beings and realized the truth. No mortal or druid kind would have survived such a happenstance to tell this tale—and yet he had. He had bargained with demons from the underworld, and now his one and only desire lay within his reach.

Fiana. For so long her name had been a curse upon his heart. Now it became his every dream again. *I shall soon have you in my arms once more.*

As Galan emerged from the passage, he

dismounted and saw no one. For the first time in centuries the entrance to the enchanted forest stood unguarded. Only a pair of torches burned above mounds of flowers placed on either side of the tunnel. Another insult, for he knew it had not been prepared for his return. The Moss Dapple had paid tribute again to those facking Pritani. Well, at least it would be the last time.

As disrespectful as it was, it relieved him to see none of the tribe standing in homage. Doubtless they had gathered around the evening meal fire and made some ridiculous offering ritual to beseech the Gods. Fair journey for the Mag Raith and that slut.

Fair likely not, but short it would be, straight from their abandonment of the tribe into the merciless clutches of the Sluath.

The turn of events had been a perilous one, but nothing could have made him happier. He would ask to watch as they were slain by their demon masters. He particularly wished to see their claws reduce Domnall mag Raith to a screaming, writhing pile of torn flesh. Then, after Iolar resurrected Fiana, Galan would wheedle from the Sluath the secret of immortality. Perhaps he'd even promise them his idiot tribe in exchange.

Refreshed by the prospect of such fine justice, and the boon the Mag Raith had never given him, Galan took his mount to the tribe's stables, where he handed him off to the brother in charge of the beasts. The other druid said nothing, and only glanced at him before guiding the horse to its stall.

Annoyed, Galan walked out and followed the path to the settlement. Doubtless Aklen, ever the purest of souls, would have stern words for him. He would let the shaman scold while he considered what he would require for his pursuit of the Pritani. He had already decided on which mount he would take when he saw the shaman standing with the tribe's elders. They waited directly in front of his cottage, each holding a golden scythe.

Druids never wielded scythes except in the presence of an enemy. Must he teach them even the most basic of proper defenses?

"Brothers." He took in their expressions, which ranged from sorrowful to stern. "I followed the Mag Raith in hopes of persuading their return, but they eluded me in the hills. I shall attempt to track them on the morrow."

"We've accepted they should no' return, Galan Aedth." Aklen stepped forward. "We but hoped you wouldnae."

"I'm headman of this tribe." The words fell flat, even on his own ears, as Galan realized why they were armed. "My guidance has kept our people safe since the time of the invaders."

"You deceived the tribe as well as the Mag Raith, Aedth," the elder with the sternest face said. "You've kept our people terrified with your tales of fickle Gods and unknown enemies, and imprisoned our settlement against a threat that 'twould seem doesnae exist. By thus you cut off the Moss Dapple from the rest of druid kind. 'Tis unforgivable, what you've done."

He thought of the hordes of Sluath that had emerged from the mist, and smiled thinly. "I might now prove my claims, Brother, but you wouldnae survive it."

Aklen shook his head. "We ken now the face of your lies, and yet you persist. Collect what you wish to take, Aedth, and begone with you. The Moss Dapple banish you from the tribe, in this and all future incarnations."

Galan imagined squashing the shaman with a crushing spell. Hearing his skull crack and watching his brains spill out seemed almost worth his own certain, subsequent disincarnation by scythe. But Prince Iolar's promise to him had made all that he had once valued seem now as meaningless as dust beneath his boots.

"I want naught from you but a horse," he told Aklen. "Have it saddled and ready for me at the falls passage."

Inside his cottage Galan collected enough garments and provisions to last him as he tracked the Pritani. To the pack he made sure to add the most powerful of his potions and spell scrolls, carefully stowing the precious vials where they couldn't break. On his way out, he stopped by the hearth, and took from the mantel an old, small shell pendant carved with the face of a woman with striking features and kind eyes. He'd had to replace the fine chain that held it many times. The tiny carving had almost been worn away by the centuries he'd spent holding and caressing the only likeness of Fiana.

"Soon, my love," he murmured, pressing the pendant to his lips. Hanging it around his neck, he glanced at the banked fire in the hearth. "Naught else matters."

A few moments later Galan shouldered his pack and walked out, passing Aklen and all of his people as he left the settlement. He didn't glance back at the tribe he had ruled since his wife's death. They believed they had banished him, but in truth they had set him free. The shaman did not follow him, but soon after the smell of smoke grew thick.

At the tunnel passage Galan mounted the horse left tethered there for him, and looked one last time toward the settlement. He could see the glimmer of the flames now, and the plumes of smoke rising as his cottage burned.

Chapter Thirteen

F inding the old stronghold vastly
changed and yet fallen in ruins cast a
pall over the hunters, one that
Domnall silently shared. He'd been a fool to
expect Dun Chaill to have survived as he
remembered it, and doubted any trace of their
first stay still existed. Over time invaders must
have occupied the place and built onto it
before they abandoned it, for the ruins of
what had once been a small fortress appeared
vastly enlarged. The forest had gradually
reclaimed the place, clustering around and
then growing within the moss-splotched walls.
Once the roof had collapsed, the interior
became planting grounds for any falling seed,
and now possessed trees that had grown

higher than its many towers. Every other wall he saw had decayed badly, and black gaps appeared where stones had been pried out or weathered away by the wind.

Whatever the morning sun brought to light, Domnall suspected, it would do nothing to help the Mag Raith find the truth of their past.

Putting the hunters to work making camp for the night, Domnall gathered dry deadfall and made a small fire so that Jenna might warm herself. Only then did he realize he hadn't seen her since coming out of the remains of the gate house.

"Mael," he said as the tracker brought stones to ring the flames. "Where's the lass?"

"Last I saw Jenna, she told me she wished to look at something and headed in that direction." The big man jutted his chin toward the partially-collapsed tower yet standing beyond the heap of another flanking the outer gate walls. "She went quickly, but 'tis expected since we didnae stop but once." When Domnall frowned at him, he sighed. "You didnae have sisters, Overseer. The lass likely wished to see to her needs."

"Dinnae call me Overseer," Domnall said but caught Mael's expression. "I'm but a Pritani hunter again, no more."

"You're our headman now," Mael corrected. "Surely you'll answer to that."

Nectan had been long dead, but without a tribe he had no claim to the rank. Then he recalled what Galan had once called Brennus, the leader of the Skaraven Clan.

"Mayhap Chieftain."

"Chieftain of the Mag Raith," the tracker echoed, and nodded as if satisfied. "Aye, 'tis more fitting." He placed the last of the stones and went to gather more.

Domnall fed the flames, but every passing moment increased his displeasure. He'd given Jenna his dirk, and knew her sensible enough not to stray far. Still, since entering the forest he'd felt uneasy. The land had gone wild, and predators likely roamed at night. Even if the lass didn't know the dangers, she should not have gone wandering alone in the dark.

"If 'tis gnawing at you, Chieftain, go after her," Mael advised him when he returned. "She'll surely be finished by now."

Domnall lit a torch and headed toward the

half-fallen tower. Along the way he saw signs of Jenna's tracks in the scatterings of dead leaves and twigs on the ground. Her trail led him to the base of the tower, where a narrow, rough-edged gap appeared in the mossy stonework. Beyond it three low walls enclosed what might have been a garden, but now looked like a graveyard of half-buried, rotted timbers.

"Jenna?" he called out, keeping his voice low as he peered through the fall of ivy inside the gap. "Call back to me."

"Up here."

Domnall looked up to see her high above him, leaning slightly over the very top edge of the tower wall, a wall from which bits of rock and dirt now sifted to shower the ground. Dread filled his veins and stabbed him in the heart, making it difficult to speak with calm.

"'Tis no' safe, lass. Come down now."

"It's not as bad as it looks." Unaware of the precariousness of her situation, she sounded like any excited bairn. "From up here I can see most of the inner ward. The trees outside the walls block the interior view. Some of the biggest sections look as if they're still intact."

If he dashed up after her, he might bring the whole tower down. Never taking his eyes off her, he crouched and planted the torch in the ground. His hands needed to be free if he was to catch her. Though his jaw clenched tight, he forced his voice to stay even as he stood.

"Aye, and doubtless they'll still be thus by morning." He jabbed his finger at her and then at the ground.

"Right." Jenna grinned. "Coming down now."

The knot in his chest loosened with every step he heard from within as she descended. The ivy dragged at her hair and shoulders as she emerged, and she paused to free herself before stepping outside.

"It's enormous," she told him, again sounding delighted. In the torchlight her face looked flushed with pleasure. "There were at least six, maybe seven towers—"

Domnall snatched her off her feet and held her at his eye level, to be sure he had her attention. "You shallnae plague me by wandering off thus. Ever again."

"I told Mael." She tried to wriggle free, and then frowned when he held onto her. "Are you planning to carry me like this back to camp?"

"Quiet." He carried her until he pressed her back against the solid stonework of the tower. There he held her pinned as he struggled for the calm that eluded him. "I found you, and took charge of you. Protected you, fed you, defied Galan for you. I fought the facking Sluath for you. You shall do as I say."

But instead of reacting with the same heated anger, she pressed her hand to his face. "I'm sorry that I frightened you."

That she could do this to him when even his sire had been unable to shatter his control shook Domnall to his core. He lowered her to the ground, and tried to step back. But the slow slide of her body against his sent his blood surging hot and thick into his shaft. Nothing had ever felt as good as her on him, and he slid his arm around her waist to hold her there.

Jenna pressed forward against his

swelling cock, and something just as urgent flared in her eyes. "We can't do this. Not now."

He brought his hand up to the curve of her chin. "Yet we shall, I reckon. Soon."

"You don't know me." She turned her face to press her mouth to his fingertips. "I don't know me. I could be anyone, anything. Maybe even a demoness."

"Never that, lass." He pushed his thumb against her lips to keep her from arguing the point. Looking into her gaze and seeing her longing for him tempted him so that he nearly seized her up again. "Close your eyes for me. Only a moment now."

Her lashes fluttered down. "Domnall, this is...dangerous."

"Aye, and I dinnae care."

He braced his hands against the stonework on either side of her, and put his mouth on hers. Her lips felt softer than he'd ever imagined. He tasted them with the edge of his tongue, catching a trace of the spiced honey bread Mael had given her at the river. From beneath the sweetness came her own, warm and alive and luscious with female heat. When he parted her lips and took her mouth she groaned into his.

Aye, this, that I've wanted since I saw you in the grove, asleep and somehow awaiting for me. For my voice, my touch, my eyes upon you.

Jenna had spoken truth. He knew nothing of her. Yet as he kissed her Domnall knew everything. The catch of her breath, the soft sound that came from her throat, the tiny tremors that shivered through her flesh. He felt the clutch of her hands and the press of her breasts as if he'd always had such delights to relish. Her shy response, and how it grew bolder filled him with a longing and satisfaction he could never have before felt, and yet recognized as deeply and intimately as his own. By the time he lifted his mouth from hers he shook with a hunger that seemed to him he had always possessed, but locked away, waiting to be set free.

By the Gods. She's the one I've waited on, all this time?

He knew nothing of her, and yet had a shaman been within the sound of his voice he'd have called him to tie their hands with a mating cord, this very moment.

"Look upon me," he urged, and she did. "What ken you of me and the Mag Raith?"

Her damp bottom lip trembled before she caught it with her teeth then released it. "Very little. Almost nothing, except what you've told me." She touched his cheek. "But it's not what I feel."

"'Tis the same for me." Domnall turned his head to kiss her palm. "I'm but a hunter. You, lass, you're beyond all I ken."

Her eyes searched his face. "Not anymore."

❧

RETURNING to the camp site with Domnall made Jenna feel rather self-conscious at first, but none of the hunters paid any attention to them. Edane and Kiaran sat mending their saddles, and Mael crouched by the fire roasting some meat impaled on six sticks. Broden, who stood watching the forest with his usual glower, barely glanced at her.

They all suspect what we were doing, Jenna guessed, *but they're being polite.* In this tight group the only privacy they had was given as a courtesy. It made her want to hug them all. *And wouldn't that delight Broden.*

Domnall came to inspect the sticks of food. "Grouse?"

"Ptarmigan," the tracker told him. "There's hundreds roosting in the ruins. Kiaran's birds took them. I found plentiful sign of hare and quail we may snare, so we'll no' go hungry if our stores run low."

Something was wrong with what Mael said, but Jenna couldn't put her finger on it. She glanced over at the clutch of the falconer's little birds, which were all preening themselves. One stretched out its wings, making her think of the Sluath, which she didn't want to do, so she went to retrieve their waterskins.

Away from the men she also didn't have to keep pretending everything was fine.

As Jenna sorted through their packs, she did the same with her qualms. Climbing up the tower had been a little foolish, but kissing Domnall had been entirely reckless. Recent events and how she had handled them had given Jenna a sense of her own personality: focused and stubborn, and yes, even a little daring on occasion; in all things, independent and self-reliant. Yet just a few minutes ago she'd been clinging to the big man and agreeing to…what? Intimacy? A relationship? They hadn't even named it.

He didn't have to say sex. He was ready to have it with me right there against the side of the tower—and I wanted it too.

Given this outrageous attraction between them, which was only growing stronger by the day, sex seemed inevitable. But what if Domnall wanted more from her? The way he'd looked at her after that wild kiss, and what he'd said, had shaken her to her heels. She had nothing to offer him but her body. Her heart might prove as vacant as her memory.

When Jenna stood with an armful of waterskins her thigh and calf muscles locked up, sending shaky arrows of pain into her bones. She took an uncertain step before she realized she'd lifted too much weight for her tired legs to support.

"Permit me," Kiaran said, appearing at her side so suddenly she nearly dropped everything. "You shouldnae try to carry so much. You're no' a draft nag."

"You should wear a bell around your neck." She didn't mean to sound so grumpy. "Or maybe I should when I'm in a temper."

Kiaran began taking some waterskins from her arms. "When I first awoke in the ash grove without my kestrels, I felt such rage. Had they no' found me, I might have torn apart the forest out of spite."

"You got away from the Sluath with your birds?" His expression grew wary. "I didn't have anything with me when I woke up there," she added. "Not even my clothes."

"They flew after me, I reckon." He nodded at her arms. "Shall you manage those?"

Another strategic change of subject, Jenna thought, and swallowed a sigh. "Sure."

As they walked back to the camp fire Jenna still tried to piece what he'd told her into the bigger puzzle. Like the kestrels the Sluath could fly, but the Mag Raith couldn't. They'd had to ride hard all day from the Moss Dapples' lands to reach Dun Chaill. The valley had been completely exposed to the sky. Assuming the hunters had somehow escaped, how could they have gone so far on foot without getting caught? What had they used to get past the tribe's spell boundaries to reach the ash grove? Was it what erased their memories?

Could the same thing have happened to her?

Domnall and his men knew more than they were saying—or would say—in her presence. Yet Jenna was guilty of the same by keeping her ability to walk through walls from them. How were they going to get through this if they didn't trust each other?

Mael took the waterskins she held and offered her one of the spitted birds, now roasted golden brown and smelling of herbs. Yet when she sat down by the fire Jenna felt almost too depressed and heartsick to take a bite. The men would go on taking care of her, the way adults did with lost children. To them she was a burden, not a member of the group.

I kept up with them. I've done everything they've asked of me. Why don't they trust me?

"'Tis cooked through," the tracker assured her when he saw she wasn't eating.

"I'm sure it's delicious." She glanced at the stone wall and got an idea. "It's just that all the riding has tired me out." She handed the stick back to him. "I think I'd better get some sleep."

No one tried to stop her as she picked up one of the horses' saddle blankets and spread it on the ground at the base of the curved wall some distance from the fire. She stretched out and turned to face the men so they could see her, and then closed her eyes. The wall, which as she suspected provided excellent acoustics, helped her hear everything the Mag Raith said once they thought she'd fallen asleep.

"She's *taverit*, poor lass," Mael was the first to mutter. "And she'll catch chill over there."

"We've all pushed her too hard this day," Edane said. "She managed, but she's no' accustomed to riding."

That much was true. Exhaustion dragged at her, making it easy to feign sleeping. Jenna had to press her thumbnail against the center of her palm to keep from actually dozing off.

"Best take her to the nearest village, then," Kiaran suggested. "For 'tis naught out here but more hard days and cold nights, and we've no' a cart for her."

The falconer sounded heartless, Jenna

thought, but he'd treated her with nothing but kindness.

That's more about him than me.

"She stays with us," Domnall said. "I'll carry her closer to the fire, Mael."

"What more shall you do with her, Chieftain?" Broden asked, his rasping voice flinty. "For she's no' a comfort female, nor a bed slave."

Jenna inwardly winced. *He's as blunt as a club.*

"She'll choose what she's willing to give me, and when, Brother," Domnall said flatly. "Only ken that I shallnae refuse her."

A short silence fell over the men after that, until Kiaran said, "I let it slip that my kestrels found me in the ash grove."

"We should tell her all," Edane said. "Mayhap then she'll confide the same in us. I've seen her looks. She's quick, so she's likely guessed much."

"'Twill wait until we've fathomed more of this place," Domnall said. "Kiaran, stand half-rise watch. Broden next, then wake me for the set watch. Mael, you'll have charge of the lass. Dinnae permit her enter the ruins again. I found her atop that half-standing tower."

"Let us talk of the battle," Broden said, followed by murmurs of assent.

It was the last thing Jenna heard before she lost the fight to stay awake.

Chapter Fourteen

✦❀✦

Shadows cloaked Cul as he kept watch from his perch in the north tower. Had the six intruders been mere mortals he would have killed them. Part of him yearned to add their bones to the pile of every other blunderer to trespass on his lands since his possession of the fortress. This time he could not.

These men looked human, but they smelled of the underworld and the sky. Since they could not be as he was, that meant they had been transformed. It also suggested something far more important to Cul: they had escaped those who had changed them. His twisted lips parted, and his sigh wafted out through the jagged labyrinth of his teeth.

Even now he knew their masters would be hunting them.

At long last the time had come for his justice.

Immensely pleased by the prospect, Cul regarded the sleeping mortal woman. Unlike the men she had not been improved, and her mortal scent made his blood run hot. He could kill her with but a twitch of his hand, or linger at the work and bathe in her agony. Yet her death would alert her companions to his presence, and that he could not permit.

He also felt a grudging admiration for the plucky little female. Of the six only she had dared to enter the east tower, and climb to the very top of the steps. He'd seen how her face had changed as she gazed upon his home. When she had gone down to speak to the largest of the men, she had spoken of Dun Chaill as if it were a treasure instead of a ruin.

That endeared her to Cul, who felt the same.

After banking their fire three of the men lay beside it to sleep. Another climbed an oak overlooking the encampment, likely to stand sentry. The big one who seemed to be the leader now picked up the slumbering female and put her between the fire and the next-largest male. He went to the opposite side to sleep, but watched the female for a long while before he closed his eyes.

The leader felt strong desire for her, Cul decided, and yet did not know why. Another interesting wrinkle that suggested why the men had come to Dun Chaill. They searched for answers to questions they could not know to ask. Like all their kind they behaved as wayward foundlings, stumbling through the world as if unaware that it held the most appalling dangers. From what he had over-heard they had also kept what they did know from the courageous little female.

I could tell them all, Cul thought. *See what such fine, brawny males think of the truth behind their transformation, and the nature of the female they so nobly protect. How amusing it would be to see the horror in their eyes before I slaughtered them. To hear her scream as she watched.*

Just as his own mother had shrieked the first time she had looked upon her younger son.

Moving through the castle soundlessly by

long habit, Cul left the north tower without drawing the intruders' attention and entered the pantry. Collecting the stores he needed to move below ground required several trips, and the task annoyed him. He'd just brought everything above after the thaw to enjoy the fair weather, and resume his watch from the tower. Now he would have to slink away again to hide in the darkness and attend to his work.

Once he transferred what he would need Cul safeguarded his chamber, but he could not rest.

Beneath the ruins a maze of tunnels ran from all that he had built during his long occupation of the fortress. Now he walked them, his eyes again growing accustomed to his dark world. He stopped at the chamber where he had long ago found his own freedom. Pressing his scarred brow against the door, he rubbed it back and forth as he recalled what the leader of the men had said to the female.

You're beyond me.

The scent of blood stopped his mindless self-torment, and he stepped back to look upon the wet smear he'd left on the door.

"No longer," Cul murmured. It had been

so long since he'd spoken aloud his voice came out thin and reedy, and the sound of it made a raucous growl spill from his throat. It took him another moment to recognize it as laughter. "You're no longer beyond me."

He climbed up one last time to make use of a spy hole to look upon the camp. All but the light-haired sentry now slept. By dawn they would awaken and come into the ruins to look for their answers. The little female would be first to enter, he imagined.

The effort he had spent in perfecting his castle had sometimes felt wasted, but no more. He had not labored in vain. What had begun as a much-needed sanctuary had become his greatest masterpiece. In time the intruders might even discover a few of its many secrets. Inwardly he grinned.

If Dun Chaill allows that.

Chapter Fifteen

✦✦✦

At first light Domnall ended his watch by kindling a new fire atop the embers of the old. The work gave him time to look upon Jenna without the watchful eyes of the other hunters. She slept as she did everything: quietly. To see her asleep brought something to rise in his chest that felt almost as keen as a blade wound.

She should be in my arms, that I might feel her breath on my face.

The crackling of the wood quickly roused the other men from their slumber, and Domnall turned his attention to the morning tasks. He sent Edane to check on the horses, and Kiaran to fetch more firewood. Mael heated small stones to add to the largest waterskin, along with a handful of herbs and berries to make up a morning brew. Broden collected the blankets, stopping only when he reached Jenna, who still slept on.

"There's a tangle," Mael murmured, nodding at the trapper as he retreated. "He'll no' spare the lass a kind word, yet cannae bear to wake her."

"Dinnae prod him." Broden's surly warning last night had made Domnall realize the other man felt protective of Jenna, not that he would ever admit it. He glanced down at the steam drifting from the skin's spout, and another concern occurred to him. "How much water and food have we left?"

"Twoday's rations, but we've plenty to hunt." The tracker grimaced. "If we dinnae find water, our skins shall empty by the morrow."

Riding back to the river would take too long, and put them at risk of being spotted if the Sluath had managed to track them. Whoever had built the first fortress had likely dug at least one well for a secure water supply. That was likely now buried under great layers of forest doss or rubble, or gone dry.

Domnall looked up at the white peaks of the mountains. Where there was snow, there would be meltwater. No one built a castle out of a fortress without water close enough to haul to make mortar, cool their forge and keep their builders' thirst quenched.

"We'll search for a river or lochan."

"I heard sounds of currents from there in the night," Broden said as he joined them, and pointed toward a thicket. "Walk with me, and we'll look."

Domnall accompanied the trapper through the brush and into a broad swath of old oaks. On the other side of the trees the land spread out, hemmed by a fast-running stream. The sparkling waters snaked around broad, flower-speckled glens and lush green pastures that stretched for leagues in three directions. Sheep and goats grazed across the southern-most corner, suggesting a farm or village lay within droving distance.

The signs of settled people eased some of Domnall's other concerns. They would need to barter for what they couldn't hunt or fashion themselves. The mortals might also know who had occupied and enlarged the old fortress, and what had happened for them to leave it to ruin. He also suspected that finding water wasn't the reason his trapper had asked him to accompany him.

"What weighs on you, Brother?"

"'Tis much changed, Dun Chaill," Broden said, watching the animals. "Gone strange in some manner I dinnae ken, and no' just from the vastness added to it. I keep watch over my shoulder, and on my every step. Do you reckon I'm fashed?"

Domnall shook his head. "I've felt the same, even as we rode from the pass."

The trapper crouched down to collect a handful of pebbles. Rising, he began dropping them one by one into the stream. "That fack Galan didnae lie about our prospects. We've no tribe left, nor allies outside the Moss Dapple's lands. We've naught but what remains of Dun Chaill. 'Twill aid us to protect ourselves and your wench. But we should first learn what 'twas done to make the fortress into a stronghold, and why."

"That and who might now hold claim to the place." He needed to make one thing clear to the trapper. "I didnae speak as I should last night of Jenna. I've no claim to the lass, Broden, but I want her, and no' as my wench."

The tracker said nothing for a long moment. "She's no' like us."

"Even so." He'd have a mortal lifetime to share with her, which seemed better than nothing.

"Then forget my counsel to you at the river," the trapper said, and tossed the remaining stones into the water. "Tell the lass how we're changed. Why we dinnae hunt unless we must." He regarded him. "She should ken the man she offers herself to before she declares it."

Now Domnall understood the trapper's change of heart. During their mortal lives Broden's looks had drawn many lasses to him, but only one had managed to catch his eye in return: Eara, the beautiful daughter of the tribe's war master.

Broden had not encouraged the lass, but he'd often watched her when he thought no one would notice. Although her parents did much to keep Eara from the trapper, the lass decided she wanted no other as her mate. She declared as much to Broden's sire when he came to trade with the Mag Raith. Unhappily she'd spoken to him openly during an evening gathering of the entire tribe.

"Wed yerself to my son? Be ye daft?" The headman had laughed heartily at Eara before making a contemptuous gesture toward Broden. "He's my slave's bastart. He'll never have lands nor rank. Ye'd do better to mate with a pig herder, lass."

Eara had fled weeping, Domnall remembered, but Broden had remained. His unfortunate origins finally confirmed, the trapper had borne the tribe's stares and murmurs without flinching. He'd done the same the next moon, when Eara had been wed to her sire's choice, the tribe's dour, hulking stonemason.

"She'll ken the truth first," Domnall told the trapper. "And I'll abide by what Jenna wishes after 'tis made plain."

"She'll want you," Broden predicted, sounding slightly appeased, and then glanced up at the brightening sky. "Only remember what wants *her*."

THE WARMTH of sunlight on her face woke Jenna from a deep, dreamless sleep. She opened her eyes to see Mael crouched by the camp fire and pouring the steaming contents from a waterskin into a row of cups. From the pungent and minty smell she guessed he'd made another brew, but how he'd heated it without burning the skin puzzled her. Then she saw the droop at the bottom, as if something heavy had been added to the contents, and the heap of small pebbles on the fire stones. They reminded her of the pile of rubble she'd skirted last night to reach the dirt-glutted stairs inside the tower.

They don't fit.

Jenna sat up and immediately bit back a groan as every sore, tight part of her body protested. Eyeing Mael, she said, "Good morning."

"Doesnae feel 'tis, aye?" He added a pinch of herbs to one cup before holding it out to her. "Woundwort for the rider's bruise, and water mint for your tongue."

Jenna cautiously took a sip of the fragrant brew and grinned. "Oh, that's as good as hot chocolate on Christmas morning."

The tracker squinted at her. "I dinnae ken your words."

They'd come out of her memory without any associations, except with his brew. A mild throb of discomfort pulsed between her temples.

"It must be something from my people, in America."

"Aye, 'twould seem so." He busied himself with filling the other cups. "Our tribe dwelled to the north, in a narrow valley between a loch and high mountains. We called it *Cuingealach*, the narrow pass. What call you yours?"

"Seattle, Wash– *Ow*." Pain shot through her forehead, and her hand shook as she set down the cup. "Okay, every time I remember something, it hurts worse."

"You're no' meant to think on it, lass," Edane said as he joined them. "'Tis that which took your past that pains you when you try."

Jenna met his gaze. "Do you know what's causing it?"

The archer grimaced. "I didnae finish my shaman training. The bow 'twas my only wont. But I reckon 'tis a spell of some sort." As he glanced all around them and finally over his shoulder, Jenna saw his jaw muscles working. "Aye, the feel of magic, 'tis everywhere."

A flutter of wings fanned Jenna's cheek, and one of Kiaran's kestrels delicately landed in the grass beside her. It held a small, limp rodent by the tail, which it dropped on her blanket before giving her an expectant look.

"Hello," Jenna said and pretended to admire the bird's kill for a moment. "If that's for me, little guy, then you should know that I'm never going to be that hungry."

The bird puffed up and shook its feathers from its breast to its tail before uttering a series of high-pitched chirps.

"Dive's a female," Kiaran said as he came over and bent to offer his leather gauntlet to the bird, who stepped up and clutched it with her black-tipped yellow claws. "Males have gray heads, and are no' as large." With his other hand he retrieved the dead rodent. "She's a keen one for feeding, so she'll keep bringing you voles until she sees you eat."

Mael offered her an oatcake, and Jenna made sure that the kestrel saw her take a bite. "Is she like that with everyone?"

"No," the falconer admitted. "Only the Mag Raith, and now you."

Something that felt like a hand stroking down the center of her back made Jenna look over her shoulder. From the woods Domnall and Broden emerged, both men talking in low voices until they saw her. Then both fell silent and the trapper avoided her gaze.

Looks like I'm the topic of conversation again, but why?

Another, lighter sensation slid down along her spine, and she saw the overseer in the next moment rub his inked arm. She followed the heavy bulge of his bicep up to his shoulder, and then saw the tic of his pulse just below his jawline. Her breath caught as her gaze shifted up to lock with his, and she lost herself in the golden emerald wildness of his eyes.

We should be naked and alone.

All the sounds around Jenna seemed to grow distant, and the heat of the early morning sun sank into her skin like warm water. She could feel in her throat the heavy thud of a strong, deep pulse. Her own heart sped to a frantic, trapped-moth beat, and all the breath slipped out of her lungs. Somehow

Domnall was doing this to her, and he didn't appear to be aware of it. As he came closer his scent flooded her senses as if he were on top of her instead of a dozen yards away.

If he'd been within reach Jenna would have flung herself at him.

The strange enchantment ended a moment later when Domnall took his hand from his arm, and Broden called to Edane to help him lead the horses to water. It almost hurt to feel it vanish from her, as if she were losing part of herself. To feel that way about a man she'd known for only a few days should have shamed her, but she didn't care. Whatever it was, she wanted more.

"I've some borage if the woundwort doesnae help," Mael said to her, breaking the spell.

"No, this is good." Feeling flushed, Jenna pushed the erotic thoughts out of her head and quickly finished the brew. She stood and went still, looking down at her legs. "More than good. I feel great."

The tracker frowned at her, and then nodded. "Aye, the brew, 'tis never failed me."

"Good morning," Jenna said as Domnall

approached her, hoping she wouldn't end up in another erogenous trance. "Can I help with the horses, or are we going to explore the castle?"

"'Tis signs of a settlement to the south." He spoke to Mael, not her. "We'll ride there with the lass to barter for what's needed. Kiaran, you, Edane and Broden shall guard the camp."

The falconer lifted his arm, from which Dive flew, and then handed Mael a sack.

Jenna frowned as Domnall walked off toward where they'd hung their saddles last night. "Shouldn't we have a look around first before we decide to stay here?"

"'Tis decided, lass," Mael told her as he opened the sack and took out a brace of ptarmigan. "Domnall's our chieftain now. We abide by his rule."

"I don't." Even as she said that Jenna felt idiotic. "Please understand, I'm grateful for what Domnall and all of you have done for me. I doubt Galan would have let me live. But I'm not Mag Raith. I'm…I'm American."

The tracker's brows rose. "You're no' in

America anymore, lass. You're here, and Domnall's our leader. He's a good and fair man. You've naught to fear in accepting his charge."

"I'm not afraid of him." Frustration knotted inside her as she tried to find the words to explain her feelings. "It's just that…I don't know. Maybe my people don't have a chieftain or headman."

"Of course, they do, lass," Mael said. "Och, dinnae give me such a glower. You've but forgotten the way 'tis for every tribe."

If she kept trying to remember she'd give herself another headache, so Jenna simply nodded and finished her oatcake.

They started out a short time later, riding through the forest and crossing the stream Broden had found. On the other side the land sloped down before it spread out into the valley. When she looked back at Dun Chaill she couldn't see any part of the castle. The forest had swallowed it up completely. Watching the trees as they passed allowed her to pick out another oddity.

"Someone planted those oaks over there," she said to Domnall, and pointed to the most visible rows at the forest's edge. "They look smaller than the others."

He reined in his mount and scanned the tree line. "Mayhap they wished to replenish what they felled for building or burning."

"But why take it from here? You'd have to drag the logs through the forest." Then she realized something else. "There aren't any stumps."

Domnall regarded her. "You see trees like the *dru-wids*."

"Or maybe I've chopped down a lot of them." The thought of even belonging to the same kind of tribe as Galan made her suppress a shudder. "What do you think, Mael?"

"I reckon we should ride now," the tracker said, "and fathom such after our return."

Chapter Sixteen

Acutting wind greeted Galan once he'd finished his search of the settlements nearest the Moss Dapple's lands, and howled after him as he rode up into a maze of rocky, barren slopes. Once he reached the appointed meeting place, he dismounted and hobbled his horse. As a precaution he cast a ward over the horse to keep it from bolting when the Sluath arrived. He then did the same to protect himself, and slipped a vial containing a blinding potion into his sleeve.

Prince Iolar might possess powers far beyond anything imaginable, but to use them he'd surely need eyes to see.

Standing on an outcropping to keep watch

on the sky, Galan silently debated how much
he would ask of the prince. Despite his efforts
he'd been unable to find a trace of the Mag
Raith, which suggested that they had either
fled or gone into hiding.

While serving the tribe, the hunters had
suppressed their savage Pritani natures, but
their brutish ways could never truly wane.
Even confronting creatures as terrifying as the
Sluath, Domnall and his men were unlikely to
run. Galan knew his former defenders would
wish to answer the unexpected attack out of
pride, but they'd use their keen instincts and
experience as hunters to safeguard themselves
while they prepared to strike back.

He felt sure that they had gone to ground,
to hide and watch and scheme with that dark-
haired slut. But where?

A blast of needle-fine ice pelted his neck,
and Galan turned to see the radiant figure of
the Sluath prince emerge from the nearest
cave. Wings of gold-tipped white spread out,
huge and magnificent, shedding swaths of
frost crystals. Yet in a blink they folded in on
themselves and disappeared. A shimmer of
barely-perceptible   magic   cloaked   Iolar,

reshaping his unearthly form with the illusion of a tall, fair-haired mortal warrior.

Seeing the transformation again made dread grip Galan's throat, keeping him mute as the prince approached him. He'd had to wonder if, in his rage, he'd imagined the unearthly creatures. But now any doubt that lingered over the existence of the Sluath dissolved. As he looked into Iolar's golden eyes, his bladder swelled as if hot and loose, and he but a quailing, quivering lad facing a monster.

Show naught of it.

"Fair day, my prince." He bowed low enough to show respect, but not so deeply that he pissed himself. "I didnae ken your kind use the caves."

"We don't, Druid," Iolar said as he stepped closer. He raised a languid hand to probe the space between them. "You've shielded yourself. How tiresome you humans are. Where are the hunters?"

"I cannae yet tell you." Galan slipped his hands into his sleeves, and uncorked the vial. "'Tis a large territory I must search. To find them I must hire men to aid me. I've no' the means to do thus." When the Sluath said nothing he added, "I need gold."

"Gold that you expect me to provide." The prince moved closer, stopping only when the protective ward crackled. "Very well." His eyes never left Galan's. "Danar."

Another, larger Sluath emerged from the cave, and tossed a bulging leather pouch to Iolar, who caught it without looking back. He dropped the purse at Galan's feet before he thrust his hand against the ward. Power flashed, and shards of ice sprayed in all directions, but the magic held.

Iolar snarled, baring snow-white teeth. "You dare deny me."

"I cannae find the Mag Raith if I'm made your fodder," Galan told him, and wondered if the ward would survive another such blow. "Keep to our bargain, and you shall soon have back your hoor." The Sluath said nothing. "I'll leave this territory to hire the men and continue the search. How shall I find you?"

Iolar reached back and yanked at something, returning his hand with a gilded white feather. "Burn it, and I shall come to you." He threw it to the ground.

Galan knew better than to risk breeching his ward to reach for the gold or the feather. "I shall find them soon, my prince."

Iolar turned away, creating a snow flurry as his wings smashed through the illusion of his mortal guise. He flew past Danar into the cave, which glowed briefly.

"Don't fail him, Druid," the big Sluath warned. "For I'll peel you slow, and choke your screams with the skinnings."

Galan waited until the light from them both faded from the interior of the cave. Only then did he drop his ward. He ignored the spreading dark patch from his bladder as it stained the front of his robes. Quickly he collected the gold and the feather, and went to retrieve his mount.

Chapter Seventeen

❧❦❧

Domnall led the way along the edge of the valley taking note of scant evidence of old trails leading into the slopes that they passed. The ridges appeared empty, and judging by the over-growth and rocky conditions none of the paths had been used for some time. The deep sods and untouched look of the valley's grazing lands also baffled him. Such rich, fertile land would be prized among stockmen, yet it appeared only the deer herds made use of it.

Along the way Mael showed Jenna the different tracks of animals that had recently traversed the valley. Domnall dropped back to ride alongside them as the tracker explained how the patterns of movement helped hunters predict where they would congregate, and why.

"Stags look for hinds, females, to breed before the snowfall," the tracker said. "The herd stays in the valley for winter where it's warmer. By now all the hinds have birthed, so they'll be in the slopes with their calves."

"I saw two deer with antlers by Domnall's cottage," she told him. "Those were both stags, right?"

"Aye, for the males congregate until the rut begins again." Mael winked at her. "The hinds'll want naught to do with them until then."

Jenna smiled a little, and then regarded Domnall with a look that made him wish they were alone. Never had a female entranced him more with a simple gaze.

White smoke drifted ahead of them, and made him rein in his mount.

"Hold," he ordered.

He eyed the source of the plume, a narrow gap in the slopes. He could also see a high, well-built drystane wall stretching across the valley between them and the grazing animals.

From the amount of moss pelting it, the wall had stood for decades.

"They put up stone," Mael murmured under his breath, sounding perplexed.

"What's wrong with that?" Jenna asked him.

"'Tis far more work than needed," the tracker said. "Our tribe planted hedges of hazel to enclose pastures in but a season. That..." He nodded at the wall. "...took much spine-cracking work."

No shepherds or herding dogs occupied the pasture, but the loose condition of the sheep's long fleeces told Domnall they were ready for rooing. The animals also showed a healthy amount of fat, suggesting they'd been regularly grazed since the cold season.

He scanned the slopes again but saw nothing to make him wary. "Keep watchful, Tracker."

Slowly they rode up to the wall, and Jenna turned her head to peer down the length of it.

"Whoever built this knew their trigging," she murmured, reaching out to touch the rough surface of the stacked rocks. "They chiseled wedge stones to fit in every single gap."

"'Twas no' built of late," Mael said. "From the weathering and signs of repair I'd reckon 'tis stood for centuries, as Dun Chaill."

"I don't think the castle builders constructed this," Jenna told him. "This wall was made with schist and flagstone, probably gathered from rockfalls at the base of the ridges. Dun Chaill's walls and towers were made of quarried sandstone and granite."

Domnall might have attributed her knowledge to hearing it spoken by a stone-cutter sire or mate. But Jenna spoke with the easy assurance of someone who had worked with such stone and knew how it had been acquired. It also explained her immediate fascination with Dun Chaill: she had likely designed such places in her past. Yet he suspected that whatever her tribe, no female in Scotland would have been permitted to do such work.

Combined with all the other oddities Jenna possessed, Domnall wondered if she might be *dru-wid* kind after all. Only the tree-knowers could do one thing that ordinary folk could not: reincarnate and travel through the ages.

"Look here," Mael said, distracting him from his startling thoughts.

Domnall saw on the other side a well-worn path leading from the pastures into the gap, and looked ahead to see smoke rising in the distance. A heavy wooden gate overgrown by brambles connected the wall to one side of the slope, completing the barrier.

As they drew closer Domnall saw the brambles had been stripped of their berries and leaves, and woven like bracken to cover the gate with thorns. Atop the protective layer small chunks of white and pink quartz wound in twine had been tied to form a three-sided spiral. The *dru-wids* used similar arrangements of crystals to maintain their protective wards around the enchanted forest.

"'Tis been charmed," he warned Mael.

"Aye." The tracker eyed the heavily-covered gate as he dismounted and carefully reached into the thorns. "But no' against us."

A rusty sound came from the gate just before he tugged it open.

Domnall rode ahead, deliberately putting

space between him and Jenna and Mael. He knew the tracker would keep close to the lass and, if necessary, turn and ride off with her at the hint of a threat. On the other side of the wall he saw deep heaps of ash and charred weeds from fires built so near the stones many bore scorch marks. He recognized the bits of purple-splotched stalks as poison, and kept one hand on his sword hilt as he passed through the gap and emerged into another, smaller glen.

Inside a wide circle of flourishing gardens and crop fields stood a small village of well-kept cottages and sheds. Several women in the three-sided green at the center worked over steaming wash pots while children played nearby on a bench. A number of men led pairs of yoked oxen out of a barn. On either side of the road leading into the settlement two round, peak-roofed poultry houses stood with large slatted window openings.

Domnall realized why they'd been positioned there when a half-dozen geese poked out their heads and began uttering raucous honks, stopping the villagers at their labors. The women retreated at once, taking the children with them. The men with the oxen stared at him, their surprise plain.

Domnall dismounted. Signaling Mael to keep his distance, he drew his sword and went down on one knee. Holding the blade parallel to the ground to show that he meant no harm, he waited.

Two young, muscular cottars came out, both holding hoes on their shoulders.

"What do ye here, stranger?" one of them demanded.

"I'm but a traveler passing through this valley with my kin." He gestured behind him. "We've come to trade, if you'd welcome it."

The cottars peered around him and then eyed the brace of ptarmigan Mael had attached to his saddle. They muttered to each other for a moment, and then let out two sharp whistles.

An older man wearing finer garments came to join them. "'Tis well, lads. Be off with ye." To Domnall he said, "Ye cling to aulden ways."

"'Tis best remembered in strange lands, *Maister*," he told him. "You're the headman?"

The older man nodded. "Rise, lad. Ye'll come to no grief here in Wachvale."

"I'm grateful." Domnall planted the tip of his sword in the ground before he stood. "Have you trouble here?"

"Guard against it." The headman looked past him at Jenna and Mael, and some of the tension left his features. "We've no inn nor tavern, but ye may trade in the green, and there water yer mounts."

"I saw burnt hemlock by your wall beyond," Domnall said as he flipped the dirt from his blade and sheathed it. "'Tis to safeguard the sheep?"

"Aye, and the village." Without further explanation the older man turned and walked away.

Chapter Eighteen

All that morning Edane couldn't shake the feeling that something had gone missing. He walked around the camp three times as he counted packs and horses, but found nothing lost. His disquiet added to the unease he'd felt since arriving at Dun Chaill. The old fortress that had once been their refuge now seemed like a great, slumbering beast. Though Broden and Kiaran went about their tasks with hardly a glance about them, Edane felt as if the castle's ruined towers were somehow watching him, their jagged shadows growing longer with the passing hours.

"I'll set snares down by the water, and gather rushes to dry," Broden said once they'd

finished collecting and stacking enough firewood to last them several nights. "We'll want
greens for the meals if Domnall cannae trade
for them."

He eyed Edane with an arched brow.

"You do it," Edane told the trapper,
annoyed by his silent presumption that he
should see to the task. He jutted his chin out at
Kiaran. "You well ken what we may eat."

"Aye, but I'm no' so swift as you to spot it.
My friends and I do better to scout the
boundary." He lifted a gauntlet as one of the
kestrels hovered over them, and the bird
dropped to perch on his wrist. "What else
shall you do? Braid Broden's fine locks
for him?"

"Naught touches the hair," the trapper
said as he began cutting strips of leather.
"Mayhap he could shave more arrow shafts, or
tromp in more circles."

Grumbling under his breath, Edane
picked up an empty sack and slung his bow
over his shoulder as he headed into the woods.
He should be hunting, not gathering veg like a
useless old crone. Yet as soon as he spotted
some tight white buds rising from a mound of

broad, pointed leaves he forgot the insult to his manhood.

Plucking the ramson leaves sent a strong odor of garlic into the air, but Edane knew they would be milder once cooked. Stuffed in birds they well-flavored the otherwise bland meat. Jenna would enjoy the taste more, and perhaps eat a little better. He felt a little foolish for worrying over her. She was Domnall's lady, not his. But her unshakeable fortitude ever tugged at him. When any other female would have begged for pity, Jenna simply kept forging on.

Edane decided to reserve some of the ramson to make a tonic for the lass, should she be plagued by bites. Insects never worried him or the other hunters, but she had such thin, fine skin, and soon the heat would bring out–

Jarred out of his musings, Edane straightened and closely studied everything around him. The winter had long fled, and the woods should have been filled with all manner of worms, midges, ants and spiders. Yet he now saw none. Since coming to Dun Chaill, in fact, he'd yet to spot so much as a single moth.

'Tis what's gone missing.

He tied the sack and began walking away from the castle toward the ridge. Halfway to the pass he finally spotted a huge web stretched between two pines, and the neatly-wrapped cocoons of the spider's many meals. As he approached it his flesh tingled along the edges, and he halted and stepped back. Lifting a hand to probe the air, Edane felt unseen power, and then saw its tell-tale shimmer. The sack fell from his hand. He'd spent too many centuries in a spell-protected *dru-wid* settlement to mistake the cause.

Someone had warded the forest with enough magic to hold back the smallest of living things. But how?

A shaman would ken.

Edane turned his back on the invisible barrier, feeling the icy bite of old shame. Never had it been his choice to serve the Gods as their instrument. He'd been born to wield the bow. He'd known it the moment he'd first watched Darro mag Raith fletching arrows for a hunt, and tried to pick one up.

No' for ye, lad. His sire had plucked him off his feet and handed him, squalling, to his mate. *'Tis a pity his size doesnae match his lungs.*

Like most Pritani men Darro stood tall
and broad, with a heavy frame padded with
great swaths of muscle suited to hard work.
Yet Edane had been born small and puny, and
sometimes fought for breath after he tried to
run. As such his worried *máthair* had always
treated him as frail and sickly. Even when he'd
grown tall, Edane remained thin, and had
been permitted to do only the very lightest
work, such as gathering. He assumed it had
been his skill in finding rare herbs that had
drawn the interest of the tribe's aging shaman.

Yer lad shall never make a warrior, but he's a fine
eye for potion makings. I've no' sired a son. Entrust
him to me, and I shall teach him all I ken.

Edane had no interest in performing
rituals and making potions. Smearing himself
with ochre and chanting before a night fire
made him feel like a pretentious fool. Yet the
old man kept insisting he had been chosen by
the Gods to serve the tribe, and warned that to
thwart them would bring down their wrath.

The Gods dinnae bestow a gift to see it thus
squandered, lad.

Pretending to hunt for herbs allowed
Edane to use the bow and arrows he'd made

in secret. That led to him hunting with Domnall and the others, and the chance to finally do as he wished. That Edane sometimes grew breathless and slightly muddle-headed he attributed to the thrill of the hunt, and of fulfilling his true destiny.

Then came the night when he'd brought a brace of hares for the shaman, and then without warning had collapsed at his feet. When Edane had finally roused he could scarcely catch his breath for what seemed to be gutting him from within.

After painting protective spirals in woad over his chest, the shaman had made him drink a bitter tonic. When his breathing eased the old man had told him a terrible truth.

Bending to retrieve his sack of ramson leaves, Edane strode away from the spell barrier. He'd never spoken to Domnall or the others of what had passed between him and the old man that night. If he had, they would never have permitted him to hunt with them again. He dimly recalled losing his breath after they'd taken shelter in the abandoned fortress, but in the next moment he'd awakened in the ash grove.

Since that day Edane had never suffered again. Yet, for what he had done, he knew himself to be the cause of their fate, as the shaman had predicted.

Ye shall be forever damned for yer defiance.

Chapter Nineteen

꧁ꕥ꧂

Riding into the village, Jenna admired the cottages and outbuildings. Unlike the primitive structures in the Moss Dapple settlement, made primarily of notched, chinked logs, Wachvale's buildings had been made with thick wattle and daub walls white-washed by chalky lime. High roofs built from layers of fern bracken and straw thatching appeared to weather well, judging by their still-solid condition. Bits of quartz crystal glittered at the top of every flagstone chimney, and boughs studded with clusters of orange-red berries hung over every threshold. The fragrant scent of baking bread and simmering soup warmed the air, adding to the aura of coziness.

The place looked peaceful and prosperous, but the villagers seemed a little nervous. Then again, the arrival of her trio was as unexpected to these people as hers had been to the Moss Dapple.

The stockmen and cotters returned to their work, but none of the women emerged from the cottages. Before coming within earshot of anyone Mael had quietly advised her to let Domnall do all the talking, and be ready to ride out if need be.

"If they were going to attack us," she murmured back, "wouldn't the first two have done that?"

"You never ken, lass," the tracker said. "Customs change, and we've no' been in the world…for some years."

Jenna eyed him, wondering what he would have said if he hadn't caught himself. Gradually she'd come to realize that everything the Mag Raith avoided discussing had to do with the passage of time. She'd also heard the headman mention Domnall using 'aulden ways.'

Just how long had Galan kept the hunters guarding the Moss Dapple?

Once they reached the three-sided patch of grass in the center of the village, Mael drew a bucket of water from the communal well there and filled a long stone trough for the horses. Domnall held up the brace of ptarmigan, turning around slowly until a pair of older women appeared. Both peered as closely at him as the birds before approaching.

"Be ye hunters?" one of them asked, while the other inspected Jenna.

"Aye, Mistress." Domnall placed the brace atop a wooden bench before taking a step back. "We'd trade these for oats and veg, and mayhap some tartans, if you're willing."

The two women's expressions turned pleasant as they came to examine the birds. Mael stayed by the horses, casually but constantly scanning their surroundings. He also kept one hand on his hip, which seemed odd to Jenna until she realized that from there, he could draw his sword quickly.

Both men obviously felt as wary as the villagers.

Why don't I?

Jenna knew her own lack of fear to be just as inexplicable. Waking up in the ash grove had felt good, not terrifying. Despite all of them being complete strangers she hadn't been frightened by Domnall, his men, or the Moss Dapple tribe. She'd deeply disliked Galan at first sight, but even he hadn't really scared her. Only the Sluath did that.

She saw one of the women beckoning to her, and walked over to join Domnall.

"Aye, as I reckoned, Hunter," the older woman said as she inspected Jenna. She tapped her crooked nose knowingly. "Too fair-faced for even a pretty lad. Wear ye trews and tunic for riding, then, lass?"

Knowing her strange accent might alarm the villagers, Jenna offered her a shy smile and nodded.

"Me daughter mated with a lowlander last season. He's a weaver, and sent more tartans than we may use. I'll fetch them for ye." The woman trotted off to one of the cottages.

"We've want of meat, but we're no' starved." The other woman gestured to one of the cotters, who brought three large sacks and placed them beside her. "One of oats, two of greens, and tartans for yer birds," she said firmly. "You'll no' get more."

"'Tis generous," Domnall said and bowed to her. "My thanks, Mistress."

The other woman returned with a bundle of colorful plaids in different patterns, which Jenna accepted with a murmur of thanks and a slightly wobbly curtsey.

"Ye're a good lass," the woman said, and then scowled at Domnall. "Only ye should do more to keep her safe. Riding through that part of the valley." She flicked her fingers in the direction of Dun Chaill. "'Tis courting an evil end."

"We passed the ruins of a castle," Domnall said, "beyond the valley. Do you ken it?"

"Aye." She made a swift circling gesture above her bodice. "'Tis cursed."

He nodded. "Have any claim now to the land? We'd camp there if no'."

The villager recoiled as if Domnall had slapped her. "Ye'd willing go back to tha' *kithan's* boneyard, ye great fool?" She gave Jenna a stern look. "Run ye from these madmen, lass." She spat on the ground before she stalked off.

"None lay claim to Dun Chaill and live," the other woman said. She grimaced before she added in a whisper, "'Tis long been the lair of a *kithan*, a naught-man. 'Twill savage any who dare enter the ruins, then strew their torn limbs across the valley." She tapped her temple with a gnarled finger. "Beheld it meself as a lass, when I herded. Three fine lads, all left in pieces."

"How long has the *kithan* dwelled there?" Domnall asked, keeping his own voice low.

"'Tis said when it came that it caught and ate alive the Mag Raith hunters, poor lads, and then hunted and killed their tribe entire." Shuddering, she twisted her hands in her skirts. "'Twas in the time of the Roms."

Jenna saw the village's headman walking quickly toward them and cleared her throat. When Domnall glanced at her, she nodded in his direction.

"See to yer work," the headman told the old woman, who quickly retreated. To Domnall he said in a much colder tone, "Ye've made your trade. 'Tis time ye go."

For a moment Jenna thought Domnall might try to persuade the man to talk to them. But he simply nodded, picked up the sacks and handed the lightest to her. After they carried them over to their horses, he tied them to their saddles before lifting her up onto the mount. She glanced over to see the headman making the same quick circling gesture over his chest as he watched them.

"Ride past the herd, and then circle back," Domnall told her and Mael. "I dinnae want them to ken our true direction."

As they rode out of the village, Domnall and Mael remained silent and stayed in front and in back of her. Only when they had gone around the sheep and turned around did Mael drop back to ride alongside her.

"Do you mean to make a gown with the tartans, and dress as a proper lass?" he asked, but the smile he gave her didn't reach his eyes.

"Maybe I'll give them to you guys." She glanced over her shoulder at Domnall's flinty expression. "If the *kithan* doesn't savage me first."

Chapter Twenty

T he valley's ripe grasses and blooming wildflowers colored the warm afternoon air with sweetness, but the ride through them back to camp only deepened Domnall's dark mood. Mael, who ever sensed such things, did his best to keep Jenna distracted. With much embellishment he spun a tale of one of their early, less than successful hunts, making light of the many mistakes they'd made as young men. While she chuckled at the proper moments, Jenna also seemed preoccupied.

Taking the lass from the Moss Dapple settlement had placed her in more danger than Domnall could have realized. She could never be left alone. What if some murderous rogue had concealed himself inside the castle, and even now plotted against them? The *kithan* the villagers feared might be but a deranged lunatic intent on slaughter without purpose or reason.

Or even worse, what if a band of brigands stumbled across her? The rare color of her eyes and the lithe grace of her form only made sure she would fetch the highest price as a slave.

Jenna reined in her mount until she rode beside him. "It's all right. The villagers think we went in the other direction. Besides that, with all their superstitions about naught-man, no one should come after us."

Any other time her voice would have soothed him, but her words proved she had little idea of what harm might be done to her.

"Ken you how to fight an attacker?" The startled look she gave him made plain how harsh he sounded. "Tell me then, what do you if a man comes at you, arms outstretched to seize you?"

"I'd run away screaming for help," Jenna said but then thought for a moment. "But if I couldn't get away from him, I'd use the blade you gave me to defend myself."

"'Tis likely he shall knock it from your fist," Domnall said and saw the frown Mael directed at him but ignored it. "What do you then, should he?"

"I don't know." Her gaze grew distant as she regarded the valley ahead of them. "I'd fight him however I could."

"A man twice your size, intent on having you?" He shook his head. "You'd fail."

"Aye, but another man with much care could teach the lass how to prevail," Mael said loudly without looking back at them. "Should one wish to."

Domnall saw the smile that tugged at Jenna's lips before she looked away, and that, too angered him. "'Tis no' a jesting matter."

"Certainly not," she agreed. "Since I can't remember how to fight, I definitely need training. Perhaps Mael will—"

"I'll train you." He regretted growling the words, especially when he saw the tracker's shoulders stiffen. "Aye," he added in a softer tone, "and with much care, as Mael says."

By that time, they'd reached the forest

surrounding Dun Chaill, where they stopped
at the stream to water the horses before
leading them through the trees. At the camp
Domnall felt gratified to see what the hunters
had gathered during their absence. Broden
had lain out peeled rushes to dry in the sun.
Edane had plentiful herbs and greens hanging
in tied bunches from a low bough. Flat stones
had been stacked over the fire, on which
bannocks now cooked.

Kiaran came out of the woods to greet
them, two of his kestrels hovering just above
his head. "Naught on the boundaries, Chieftain. Tracks of creatures, and mayhap what
'twas once a cook's garden, but 'tis long
gone wild."

"Fish abound in the stream," Broden said
and held up a string of large brown trout.
"Much hare scat and burrows are scattered
through the undergrowth. I've set snares."

"I've something for the lass," Edane said
and brought a small wrapped bundle to Jenna.
He opened it to reveal a mound of golden-red
berries.

"Thank you." She plucked one and rolled

it between her fingers. "But aren't raspberries supposed to be bigger than this?"

"They're cloudberries, lass," the archer told her. "Taste one."

Jenna took a nibble and began to wrinkle her nose, and then sighed with pleasure. "Oh, they're wonderful." She handed the bundle back to him. "But I can't eat them by myself. We should all share them."

Domnall turned away to remove the sacks from their saddles. That Edane's gift to the lass would reawaken his ire baffled him. All his hunters had come to care for Jenna. Predictably Mael had been the first to speak for her, and fretted over her still. Edane had saved her from Galan's second arrow, and calmed her after the Sluath attack. Kiaran had given up his cloak to keep her warm and charmed her with his birds. Even Broden, whose heart had surely been hewn from stone, had challenged him over the lass.

But there was one duty to her that Domnall had claimed for himself.

He took the sacks procured from the villagers to Mael. "See to their storage and give me your dagger."

Without turning to face Jenna and the rest of the men, Domnall knew he'd drawn their attention from the sudden quiet. Mael reached behind him and brought out the short blade that all the hunters carried. He placed the dagger's hilt in Domnall's upturned palm. Without a moment's hesitation, the headman spun and tossed it handle-first to Jenna.

To his surprise and pleasure, she deftly plucked it out of the air.

Edane took a half step toward Domnall. "Have a care, Brother. The lass 'tis no' a hunter."

Broden put a restraining hand on Edane's arm. "Do you no' think the chieftain kens that, archer?"

"I'll tell you what I think, trapper," Edane said without a trace of banter. "That your hand 'twill become separated from your arm if it doesnae leave mine."

Domnall pushed himself between them. "'Tis training for the lass," he said, and looked at Jenna. "We agreed, did we no'?"

Jenna stared wide-eyed down at the dagger in her hand, before lifting her gaze and focusing on his words. "Right," she said slowly, no longer sounding so sure.

"Make room," Mael said backing up.

The other men did likewise until Domnall and Jenna faced each other in the midst of the square made by the four hunters. Domnall took out his own blade from behind his back, and began circling right.

"Move," he told her. "Be my mirror."

"Be your what?" she said, watching him. "I thought you were going to show me self-defense."

A kestrel landed on Kiaran's shoulder and cocked its head at her. "'Tis what he does, lass," the falconer said. "*Move.*"

"Quickly, lass," Broden said, a warning tone in his voice. "Dinnae let him box you in."

Despite his men knowing that Domnall would sooner gut himself than see Jenna harmed, he noted that each stood in a ready stance. Centuries of being the Moss Dapple's defenders had honed their battle instincts into razor sharp reflexes.

Jenna must have sensed their tension because her feet finally moved.

"Keep the dagger up," Domnall said. "Never stop moving. Dinnae make yourself an easy target." Quickly he circled in the opposite direction, and smiled a little when she matched him. "Aye. Keep your body behind the blade."

Though she might not remember the skills of fighting with a blade, as in all else, she showed no fear. He circled a while, just long enough for her to feel at ease. Of course his brothers saw what he meant to do.

"Watch his eyes," Edane urged her as she passed in front of him.

"Keep tight hold of the blade," Mael said.

"Dinnae listen to them," Domnall said. "They but fret over–" He lunged forward, knife first.

Careful to avoid her delicate fingers, Domnall easily flicked his blade under hers with a swift, small circle. The blades tanged with a high-pitched note and in the next moment her dagger had landed on the ground.

Broden blew out a loud breath and crossed his arms over his chest. Kiaran's kestrel launched for the sky as though it had seen enough.

"Lass," Domnall said, pitching his voice

low to soothe her. "Never give up your blade. Now pick it up."

"That was an accident," she protested, her face flushed. "I didn't give it up."

But when she bent down to retrieve the weapon, Domnall stepped forward, his boot nearly landing on the blade.

"Never take your eyes from your attacker," he said.

Rather than cower away, Jenna snatched up the dagger, backed up in a crouch, and pointed the tip of the blade at him.

"Aye," Edane said. "'Tis the way of it."

Domnall nodded at her. "Good. Now slowly this time." He inched forward, gradually extending his knife arm as he made to stab at her chest. "Parry my blade by keeping your tip to the sky and sweeping your dagger across the path of mine."

As the two pieces of steel slowly met and slid across each other, murmurs of ascent came from each of the men. Domnall let her move his blade aside, but now he stood close enough to touch her. Rays of sunlight sparkled the violet flecks of her blue eyes. They gazed up into his as though she searched for something. With daggers still locked, it was as though they'd paused in some stately dance.

Only when Edane cleared his throat, did Domnall back up a pace. Jenna quickly looked away.

"Chieftain," Mael said. "We should put the mounts to graze before the daylight is lost."

"Aye," Domnall agreed.

Jenna handed his dagger back to the tracker. "Thanks for the loan," she said and started toward her horse.

"No, lass," he said to her. "Take a rest. Domnall and I shall see to them."

Following Mael out of the camp to the grassy clearing where the other mounts waited, Domnall tucked his dagger away and waited for the tracker to speak his mind.

"'Tis good we stay here," Mael said as he began unsaddling Jenna's mount. "They'd no' welcome the Mag Raith back in that village, but I'll wager Jenna may return. I reckon those two old ones would look after the lass. They might find a good, strong man for her to wed."

Domnall scowled at him, but his tracker

wasn't making a poor jest. "Aye, and when the Sluath find her? How shall those old crones or a mortal mate protect her?"

"As well as their kind may. 'Tis what Jenna is." Mael hung her saddle over a low oak bough. "You may long for what cannae be all you wish, but she's no' Mag Raith."

"No' Mag Raith?" Domnall demanded as fury flooded into his chest. He grabbed Mael's tunic and slammed him back against the weathered trunk, making the tree shake to its crown. "She wears my ink on her back."

"That doesnae make her yours, or give you the right to look at Edane as if you'd gut him for a gift of cloudberries." The tracker glanced down at his chieftain's fist. "If you cannae reckon it, next you should beat me into the dirt until I stain it red. 'Twas how my sire settled such matters with me, and my sisters, even before they could walk. Aye, and his mate, who never spoke above a whisper to him, and only then to beg him stop hurting her and her bairns." Mael met his gaze. "Well?"

Domnall released his grip on him, and looked up at the clear sky. "I've no excuse for what I've said and done. Forgive me." He held out his arm.

"Always, Chieftain." The tracker clasped forearms with him before he straightened his wrinkled tunic. "You'd do better to attend to it now, else your temper boils over in truth."

"Attend to what?" he asked.

The tracker slapped his shoulder. "'Twill come to you."

They finished untacking the mounts together, and Domnall walked back to the camp with him. Mael hailed Broden, and went off with him to check his snares. Kiaran knelt by a sapling, using it as an anchor to braid leather strips into new jesses for his kestrels. Edane had opened the sacks they'd traded for, his fingers nimbly sorting through the greens.

Jenna sat cross-legged by the fire, but rose as soon as she saw him. "Everything all right?"

Then it came clear to Domnall what Mael had meant.

"Come, lass." He went to her, and took her hand in his. "We must speak."

"Something wrong?" Jenna asked as Domnall led her around the remains of the castle's outer wall. She glanced back, but none of the others were following them. "What did I do?"

"Naught." He sounded almost detached, but his grip tightened as he led her through a gap in the wall and into a passage.

They had to go around a huge tree growing between the two stone walls. Domnall swept aside a curtain of flowery vines, revealing a curving stone arch into another passage.

"'Tis yet here."

Jenna followed him through the arch into a larger chamber lined with huge stone bins. Ferns sprang from the floor debris, carpeting the big room in feathery green fronds. Rotting timbers lay askew from where they had fallen, probably from the original ceiling. Above them innumerable vines had engulfed the few remaining beams, and now dangled long creepers in search of new anchors.

Domnall looked at everything, but his gaze kept straying back to a dirt-glutted stairwell at the far end of the chamber. He frowned at it as if it meant something.

"Is this where you and the others took shelter?" she asked, wondering if that was why he'd brought her here.

"Aye." Absently he rubbed his thumb across her knuckles. "'Twere no stairs, but a roof of ash beams and willow boughs. We found grain left to rot in the bins." He met her gaze. "Taking refuge at Dun Chaill, 'tis the last any of us remember of that night. I never wished you to ken how long 'tis been since we first came here."

Jenna knew he was trying somehow to protect her from something awful, but not knowing scared her more. "Please, just tell me."

Domnall released her hand. "'Tis been a thousand and three hundred years."

The air between them seemed to solidify into a thin glass, poised to shatter any moment, and all she could think at first was: *This is why they never talk about time.*

Reacting should have been simple for Jenna. She might have laughed at him for making such a ridiculous claim, but he wasn't joking. She'd walked through walls and water-falls. She'd watched beautiful, evil creatures flying down out of the sky to grab her. After all that she'd seen since waking up in the ash grove, believing him was easy, and yet she felt paralyzed. So Domnall and his hunters had been alive for more than thirteen centuries. They looked like men, but they couldn't be human.

Like the Sluath.

"You're saying that you and the others are…"

"Immortal," he said softly.

A soft rush filled Jenna's ears, and her head began to spin. "How?"

"I wish I could tell you. We reckon 'twas done to us in the time we cannae remember." Domnall stretched out his hand. "Dinnae fear me, lass."

"I don't know you." She took a step back, and then another. "Any of you." She turned and ran.

"Jenna, wait," he called after her.

Vines lashed her face as she fled deeper into the ruins, careening into the edges of crumbling stone and stumbling over thick roots concealed by the ferns. She knew Domnall was coming after her, she could hear his heavier steps thudding in her wake.

Jenna staggered into a hall that ended abruptly in three moss-covered walls. When she whirled around Domnall blocked her only way out. He stopped there, his hands at his sides, his expression so severe he looked like a stranger. She backed up until her shoulders struck stone, and braced herself.

"We didnae choose any of it," he told her, his voice low and rough. "We took shelter here as mortal men, and awoke a hundred years later remade as we're now, our memories of it gone. We dinnae age or sicken. Our wounds never fester but heal swiftly, no matter how grave. Our skills became beyond more than what ordinary men may do, and yet we lost all desire for the hunt. To kill for sport or plea- sure, 'tis what became detestable to us. The Mag Raith arenae Sluath, but we shall never again live as mortals."

Domnall's face wasn't angry. Though his fevered eyes glistened and his mouth twisted, it was in anguish. Jenna saw it clearly even as tears began slipping down her own face.

"Why did you keep this from me?"

"I've been selfish, to leave you unaware. So that I might be just a man with you." His fierce gaze remained locked with hers. "I want all from you, *luaidh*. I'd give you what I'm able. Yet I cannae sire a child, nor grow old with you. I'm no' a man. You must choose to stay or leave me."

Domnall stepped aside, creating enough of a space for her to pass.

Pressing her hands against the wall behind her, Jenna tried to push herself away from the stone. Instead the rough surface shifted under her fingers, and a scraping sound grated in the air as the wall began to move.

Chapter Twenty-One

✿

Smoke from greasy tallow candles made the air inside the mortal tavern murky and thick. The acrid stink of spoiled ale made a lower, noxious cloud as it rose from the spillage muddying the floor. A man growled, a maid squealed, and laughter belched through ceaseless mutterings of the gathered men. Behind a long table the big-bellied proprietor filled mugs as he listened to a red-faced drover.

As a druid would never frequent the sort of place where one found brutes for hire, so Galan had altered his appearance. Adding to his body ward the illusion of a hardened mortal mercenary had drained him, but he would attend to acquiring more power later.

For now, he had but to find the Mag Raith, and all he'd ever desired would be his again.

"Fair evening, Marster." A buxom female in a half-unlaced bodice and bedraggled skirts stepped into his path, her ample breasts straining to pop free with every breath she took. "Fetch you a bottle? We've the grandest whisky in the highlands."

"No." Galan tried to shrug off the hand she'd put on his arm, but she crimped her dirty fingers into his sleeve, determined to hold onto him. "I've business here, wench. Release me."

"Aye, Marster, but we're no' a facking kirk." Beneath the lank strands of her soot-blackened hair the tavern maid's eyes glittered with bright malice. "You come here, you drink, or my husband shall toss you out on your arse." She nodded at the fat man filling the mugs. "Ale, then?"

He stepped to one side to avoid two men who had risen to shove and shout at each other. "Bring it to the back."

Galan slipped past the brawlers to enter the adjoining room, always occupied by the tavern's less savory patrons. There he encountered a dozen men drinking and talking around the largest trestle table. He scanned their scarred faces, filthy garments and many weapons, reassured that these mortals would serve his purposes.

The tavern maid appeared and pushed a sloshing mug of cloudy ale at him. When he took it, her hand remained out. "Two groats for the drink."

Fortunately, he'd traded a nugget of Prince Iolar's gold for a sack of silver coins, and dropped two into her palm. When she kept her hand open, he realized she wanted more.

"Cannae you count?" he sneered.

"Two for the ale." She fluttered her eyelashes. "Another for drinking in the back."

Galan slapped the third coin in her hand, watched her bob and scurry off to the front of the tavern. She handed his coins over to the fat man, said something, and they laughed together, setting Galan's teeth on edge. The sooner he concluded his business, the sooner he could leave the swill hall.

He turned his attention to the men, and he waited for an invitation to join them at their table. When none offered him a seat, he took out and tossed a large chunk of gold onto the table.

The sight silenced the mercenaries. Galan drew inspiration from the tavern wench.

"Two of the same for every man who rides with me."

No one touched the gold, but an iron-haired man stood up. The scars on his face and the mashed ruin of his nose attested to a lifetime of courting violence. Beneath his blade harness his tunic bore old rusty stains in streaks—blood spatter that he'd never bothered to wash out.

"Aye, but you'll want more than company," the mercenary said, his voice as flat as his eyes. "'Tisnae so?"

"I seek five rogues who stole my horses." He moved to the end of the table so they could all look upon him. "Villagers and crofters along their path shall have seen them. Mayhap even provided sanctuary for them. I'll want them persuaded to tell me what they ken, whether they wish to or no'."

"Ah. You'll want them coaxed to spill their gullets." The man's lifeless gaze shifted around the table. "What say you, lads? Crave you a romp with herders and farmers?"

The men slammed their mugs on the table and roared their "ayes."

Galan picked up the gold and placed it in the hand of the mercenaries' leader. "I'll come for you at dawn. Have them ready to ride."

Chapter Twenty-Two

J enna jerked around to see the center of the stone wall swinging into a dark space, from which came the rushing sound of cascading water. She could see stone steps leading down into a chamber below floor level. Cool mist rose to drift around her, and she ran her hand along the seam of the stones as they grew damp.

"Incredible," she murmured, and looked up to see Domnall beside her. "Could it be a sluice or drain pipe?"

"I dinnae ken." He crouched low to peer down inside the space, and used a heavy stone to wedge the door open. "'Tis light beyond the steps, but more I cannae make out from here."

She knew he was looking at her because he

was waiting for her to say something else. He wanted her to tell him that she'd go, or stay, or simply couldn't handle what he'd become— what he was. Yet what had happened to him and the Mag Raith was no more their fault than what had been done to her. He'd accepted her as she was, with no knowledge of her life or her past. He'd left behind all he'd had for her sake. He'd told her the appalling, mind-boggling truth about what he was so that she would know everything about him before they became lovers.

Now that she knew, it made no difference. She wanted Domnall, whoever and whatever he was.

Jenna held out her hand. "Let's see what's down there." Though he looked at her hand, he didn't take it. "I'm not going anywhere without you."

The remnants of pain vanished from his eyes as he twined his fingers through hers. "You'll no' regret it, lass." He glanced over his shoulder. "Come, we must let the lads ken what you've found. They—"

Jenna slipped from his light grip, and

trotted down the steps. She wasn't going to wait for a committee to go exploring.

"Jenna, no," he called after her.

But in just a few strides, he'd caught up. "Stubborn lass," he said, catching her shoulder. He turned her so he could get past. "Stay behind me."

He stepped down, shielding her with his big body and keeping a firm grip on her hand. The stairs became steeper toward the bottom, leading them deep beneath the ruins. At last they reached the bottom, and Jenna saw what waited for them—a captured waterfall.

The castle's builders had somehow diverted a huge amount of water to flow through the top of the subterranean chamber. It emptied into a round pool with channels leading off in four directions that disappeared into ducts in the walls. Sunlight poured in from clear domes in the stone ceiling, reflecting off huge round mosaics inlaid in the pavers around the pool, illuminating the space. Both the domes and the mosaics had been made from highly-polished quartz. The refracted light caught the mist and created dozens of rainbows over the water, adding a lovely aura of enchantment to the chamber.

Domnall led her around the pool to the waterfall, and stretched out his free hand into the water. "'Tis much warmer than the stream."

"It could be coming from another source." She tilted her head back to peer at the narrow aperture at the top of the chamber. "I think the flow just started. The stonework up there is still dry and dusty in places. See the splash marks?"

"Opening the chamber entry mayhap released the water." He pointed to a mechanism, partially hidden by the cascade. It resembled a horizontal sluice gate. "I've never seen the like of it."

"Me, either." She frowned as she inspected the stone ducts carrying off the overflow from the pool. "This isn't a well. It's not collecting enough of the water." She turned her head. "They put a platform under the fall."

"Aye, for 'tis a bathing chamber." Domnall scooped her up in his arms, and carried her under the cascade, dousing them both.

Jenna shrieked and clung to him, but the

water churning over them felt as warm as a sun-splashed summer day, and quickly soaked them both. "I don't bathe with my clothes on."

"Nor I," Domnall said and shifted so that the water fell over his shoulders and back, shielding her from the spray. Droplets beaded his lashes and ran down his face as he placed her on her feet. "We should remedy that."

She smiled. "Absolutely."

Their sodden garments and boots should have made it awkward and difficult to undress, but they moved in perfect harmony. He'd already seen her in the buff, but Jenna felt as if she were unwrapping a gift as she helped him pull off his tunic. Domnall's upper torso seemed utterly flawless, completely covered in firm golden skin. The strange tattoos covering his arm contrasted sharply with his flesh, and yet now looked as beautiful to her as the rest of him. He took hold of her arms, lifting them so he could strip her dripping tunic over her head.

She wanted to hurry, but her hands lingered, stroking him from the broad yoke of his shoulders to the bunching bulges of his biceps. The moment she touched his ink she felt again that slow, delicious slide down her spine, as if they shared the same nerves. He must have felt something, too, for the smooth vault of his chest went taut.

"Do you feel that?" Jenna whispered, and then shivered as his fingers stroked up the length of her spine. "Oh, yes, that."

"Every time you move, I feel it now." He trailed his fingertips over her breasts, spreading blooms of heat and sensations so intense her nipples pebbled under his touch. "You're so soft, lass. Your skin, 'tis like new petals."

Her fingertips glided down to the banded muscle of his small waist. "You should just walk around naked." She shamelessly pressed her breasts into his hands, and slid her own around to the laces binding his trousers. It took a few moments of plucking at them before she loosened them enough to slip her hands inside. The tight mounds of his buttocks contracted against her fingers, as smooth as the rest of him. "Ah, you have to let go for a moment."

"Aye." He had her breasts cradled in his

hands by then, and was slowly sweeping his thumbs over her puckered peaks, watching as if completely absorbed. "Mayhap soon."

Jenna dropped down on her knees, taking his trousers with her, and eased them off his long, strong feet. That revealed the thick, swollen column of his erection, ruddy and laced with distended veins, right before her face. She couldn't help rubbing her cheek against the proud shaft, and would have done more but for his hands lifting her back upright.

"You'll unman me, you wee brazen wench." He jerked loose her laces and in one motion shoved her trews down to her ankles before curling his arm around her waist and lifting her out of them. He held her suspended, plastered against his chest, and she wound her legs around him. That brought her slick folds to press on his shaft, where she felt as if she were melting against him. "Jenna."

Domnall didn't have to tell her anything. She knew he couldn't wait another moment, and neither could she.

"Kiss me." She wrapped her arms around his strong neck. "Come inside me."

His mouth took hers with ravenous hunger as he clamped his hands under her bottom, and lifted her onto the heavy dome of his penis. As his tongue parted her lips, his cock forged into her pussy.

Jenna nearly came from the thrilling shock of being so perfectly kissed and penetrated at the same time, and clamped around him with all her soft, hot wetness. His body strained against hers as he plowed deeper, stretching and claiming every inch of her as his own.

Working her fingers into Domnall's hair as he filled her, Jenna curled them against his scalp. A groan from his throat met a whimper from her lips, and together made the sexiest sound to finish that first, devastating kiss.

She didn't need memories to tell her that nothing had ever been like this for her.

His chest heaved against her breasts as he held her on him. Her body felt so hot now that she expected her skin to steam, but the flush making it rosy came with waves of tingling excitement. They'd come together in the most basic, carnal way, and yet it felt so beautiful and emotional that tears stung her eyes.

Domnall pressed his mouth to her brow

before he looked into her eyes, his own glittering with fierce need and something more. "Dinnae let go of me, *luaidh*."

"Never again," she promised.

Wrapping one arm under her buttocks, Domnall held her in place as he began to draw out of her. He thrust back in, hard and deep and sure, his free hand stroking over her hip and up her waist to cup her breast. Watching her, he pumped in and out of her, his cock so hard it almost frightened her. Then the friction of his flesh inside hers flashed through her, wild and consuming and inescapable. She couldn't breathe but instead panted, and tasted his breath blending with her own. Now he was becoming her air, her earth, her world.

Images poured through her thoughts, but the aching pleasure whirled them into a chaotic blur. The tightness of their fit made them both shake and groan, but it was the way Domnall looked at her that reached into Jenna and wrapped him around her heart. She felt his skin grow slick with her sweat and the sweet, honeyed arousal he drew from her with every stroke of his hips. She buried her face in his neck and tasted the salty musk of him. She pressed her mouth against him as her body furled and tightened around him.

Every night, Jenna thought, breathless and terrified and crazy with the need for release. She'd have him every night, and every day, and every moment they could be alone and naked and together.

Nothing else could be as important as this.

Domnall tipped up her chin, kissing her again as his big body shook. He pounded into her now, heavy and swelling even bigger inside her clasping softness. His tongue drew hers into a sweet, languorous dance that belied the frantic rhythm of his fucking. Then he went so deep it jolted through her, exploding in her head and rocketing through her breasts, and everything inside her shattered into mindless bliss. At the same moment he uttered a rumbling groan and stiffened, his shaft jerking as his jetting seed bathed her pulsing insides.

Jenna held onto his shoulders, sighing into his mouth as the explosion of passion rained through her and settled into soothing embers of sweet relief. Dimly she felt her lover drop to his knees, his arms cocooning her in his heat

now. As she emerged from the depths of pleasure, she drew her hands down his arms, and
smiled as he stroked her back. Nothing had
ever felt as good as this.

But then he touched her spine, and Jenna
remembered the last hour of her life.

Chapter Twenty-Three

J enna walked into Premier Plaza's construction site that night without hesitation. One thing she'd learned while working in her male-dominated field was never to show any doubt in her own decisions. That would be viewed by her colleagues as a show of weakness, something like slicing her own wrist while swimming in a tank filled with hungry sharks.

Be clear, be firm, and find out what the blazes is going on with this job.

She'd jumped in this tank with her eyes wide open. Working for Maxwell and Associates, one of the oldest and most prestigious architectural firms in Seattle, was the first step on her career ladder. She'd been hired as an associate rather than a lead architect, but it was one step closer to the glass ceiling she fully intended to smash. Until she did, she got stuck with some lousy assignments like this one. Rumor also had it that M&A had been hemorrhaging too much cash lately, and she didn't want to end up unemployed.

Being a good sport about it, however, didn't include being made a scapegoat for someone else's screw-ups.

"Lady, you can't just wander around here," the security guard said as he trotted to keep pace with her. His long ears, heavy jowls and droopy eyes gave him the look of a basset hound in costume. "You gotta make an appointment with the super."

"I tried that."

She tilted back her hard hat and used her mobile phone to take a picture of a slightly skewed support column. No large-scale construction site ever looked pretty, but this one appeared as if a horde of squatters had taken up residence. Plaster dust, wood shavings and other material debris covered the floors. Soft drink cans, take-out boxes and cigarette butts littered every flat surface. The stench coming from a row of portable toilets suggested they hadn't been cleaned out since work began, if what Jenna was seeing could be called that.

In four weeks, Premier's owners would be expecting to rent out the building at market premium prices. Jenna wondered if charging sixty dollars per square foot would also cover a hazmat clean-up crew and tranquilizers for the tenants.

I should have come here the minute Hal dumped this in my lap.

After a month of getting nothing but vague promises for a tour once the work had progressed to a suitable stage, Jenna's patience had run out. She'd gotten stuck with this job when an overdose had put the original lead architect, Lyle Gordon, in the hospital. If she'd known that Gordon had been as sloppy with the project as his drug use, she would never have agreed to take charge.

Now she was going to see exactly how much trouble she was in. If that meant trespassing and upsetting the builders, she'd deal with it. Her name was on this budding disaster now.

"Is Junior here?" she asked, referring to the son of the construction company's owner, Rodney Percell Sr.

Lyle Gordon had landed the account when his old USC buddy Rodney Jr. had been put in charge of the work.

The guard shook his head. "Mr. Percell don't come in until around noon on Tuesday."

He was probably visiting Gordon in rehab to reminisce about all the co-eds and coke they'd shared as frat brothers. Jenna never understood people who partied their way through life. During her last year of high school, she'd lost both parents to a drunk driver, and had no extended family to support her dreams. Their small life insurance policy had paid only for their funeral and outstanding bills. After she'd been accepted to Cal-Poly, scholarships and every penny she could earn working part time had been her only safety net.

Grief had killed her social life, and by the time she emerged from it she'd become entirely focused on her education. Friends and a love life had to wait. Her future couldn't.

"You need to call Percell right now," she

told the guard as she headed for the basement access stairwell. "Tell him to get his butt down here pronto. Say his new architect is here and she's very unhappy. If he says no, then call his father."

The guard's jowls trembled. "Come on, Lady–"

"Or I'll call them before I go downstairs," she offered, taking out her phone again. "And you'll get fired for letting me roam around."

"Okay, but the lines ain't hooked up in here. I gotta go out to the trailer to make the call." He watched her head for the lower access stairs. "There's no electric in the basement."

She tugged the flashlight from her back pocket and held it up as she switched it on. "Brought my own, thanks."

Jenna used it to illuminate her path as she picked her way down the debris-cluttered stairwell, and skirted around the detritus left crowding the landings. No one had bothered to roof the stairs, so she had to step over cloudy mud puddles left behind by the last hard rain. Given that this was Seattle, that was probably ten minutes ago.

By the time she reached the bottom door
Jenna began to hope that Junior was too busy
to come down. Her boss would never approve
of her kicking a contractor's ass from here to
Tacoma.

The light steel door leading to the basement level groaned as Jenna tugged it open,
and a waft of damp air sourly greeted her.
Muddy water sluggishly flowed over the
threshold. She saw more as she slowly moved
her flashlight from side to side. More materials
had been left in haphazard piles, most of them
soaked by the flood. Countless lengths of
rebar, most of it broken, lay quietly rusting.
Swollen sacks of finishing plaster wept
congealed white ooze. The sheer waste
appalled her, and then she checked the structure and got a much bigger shock.

Every wall and column her light illuminated showed dozens of fresh cracks. Some
looked wide enough for her hand.

"Can't be." She let the door slam shut
behind her as she stepped into the shallow
water and splashed past empty palettes and
crumpled tarps to get a better look. "Junior,
what did you do?"

When she'd first looked at the initial plans Gordon had drawn up for Premier Plaza, Jenna knew that he hadn't calculated the load distributions correctly. The maximum slab load had been off so much it had taken her breath away. She'd gone directly to Maxwell, who assured her that Gordon had later corrected the error.

From what she could see Gordon hadn't done squat, and Junior had followed his flawed plans. That meant the uneven weight of the top four floors would create too much pressure on everything beneath them, including the foundation. During and after construction all buildings shifted as part of the settling process, adding more stress.

The cracks she saw all around her assured her it was already happening.

Jenna tucked the flashlight under her arm and pulled out her mobile to take more shots of the damage. Knowing this couldn't wait until morning, she called her boss at home.

"Ms. Cameron, it's ten o'clock at night." Hal Maxwell sounded tired or exasperated, probably both.

"I know, sir. It's just that I'm standing in

two inches of water in Premier's flooded basement," she told him. "And I'm seeing so much crack I should be in a drug den."

His voice immediately chilled. "I'll call Percell in the morning."

"You have to call him now. This can't wait." She approached one of the walls and touched the half-inch gap snaking from its top down to the water on the floor. "With this much damage, this place is a house of cards."

Her boss made an exasperated sound. "You're an architect, Ms. Cameron, not an engineer."

"I minored in structural engineering, sir." She'd also studied failures and collapses obsessively to learn how to build her own designs stronger and better. "No one can come back inside this building until it's been shored up and reinforced. If that's even possible."

"Very well, I'll call Percell. Stay where you are, and take as many photos as you can."

While Jenna waited, she snapped dozens of pictures, moving deeper into the basement as she did. After twenty minutes she decided she'd taken enough, and turned to head back to the stairs. That was when she spotted a tiny green light on one of the support columns, which with the lack of power made absolutely no sense.

She dialed her boss again as she slogged over to it. "I'm sorry, Mr. Maxwell, but I think someone rigged something down here."

"I'm sorry, too," he said, his voice very soft and aggrieved now. "I'd hoped that…but it doesn't matter. Please understand, it's nothing personal."

She crouched down to peer at the device. "I don't know what you mean."

"By now Percell will be there." A sigh came over the line. "Just know that the money from the insurance will save the firm. Good-bye, my dear."

Jenna stood up and stepped back as the light turned red, and then dropped her phone and ran. The muffled sounds of explosions over her head came an instant before the structure shuddered violently. Streams of dust and chunks of concrete began to rain down around her.

She almost made it out.

A few steps from the stairwell door the world fell on her, slamming her under a terrible weight. Only her head and shoulders remained untouched on the threshold of escape.

Jenna shifted in and out of consciousness. Slowly, blessedly, she grew cold and numb. She could see a small patch of night sky through the crazy jumble of rubble above her. It meant that the entire building had collapsed, and she probably wouldn't be found for days.

I don't want to die.

Golden-white light filled her eyes, making Jenna believe that she had done just that. A beautiful, ethereal creature appeared over her, his handsome face glittering with frost as his wings spread out over her. He reached down to her, and then into her, and she felt his cold hand close over her stuttering heart.

Jenna screamed.

❧

DOMNALL HELD Jenna against him as her terrible story unwound. Even as his own memories seethed inside him, he was unwilling to let her go. Her voice faltered only when she described the moment the Sluath had found her, broken and dying in the rubble.

"Everything beyond that night is still a blank, but I know who I am now." She looked up at him. "I'm from the twenty-first century. Somehow the Sluath saved me, and then brought me back through time." Her hand touched his cheek. "Do you believe me?"

He kissed her fingers. "Aye."

"I think the way that I...nearly died," she whispered. "I think it explains why I have to explore this castle. It's like something I've left undone."

Domnall helped her dress, but after he'd pulled on his own garments, he knew he could put it off no longer. He had to tell her what he'd remembered.

"Lass, I ken why the Sluath took you."

⚜

IN THE UNDERWORLD, shadows and light danced over Domnall as he paced the confines of his new cell. Hundreds of gemstones glittered from the high cave walls they studded, suggesting its former occupant had been one of the demons. All manner of sumptuous furnishings, fabrics and food, doubtless stolen from the mortal realm, had been crammed into the chamber. Opposite where the entry had been, one of their enchanted hearths crackled with white-blue flames that radiated heat and light, and yet never burned anything.

The bastarts so love their illusions.

This one suggested that he would be pampered and fed very well. A table set with golden dishes held savory-smelling roasted meats, deep bowls of colorful fruits, and mountains of pale breads. Three kegs of whisky and innumerable bottles of wine waited to be drunk in sparkling goblets. In the very center of the space stood an enormous platform strewn with silk curtains and fine linens, all in shades of snowy white, draped over a ticking that looked as soft as a cloud. Even the air he breathed had been scented with the fragrance of an exotic sunlit garden.

He guessed it to be yet another of their torments, as inexplicable as all the others they'd inflicted. He'd been tossed into pits so dark he couldn't see his hand before his eyes, and chambers so filled with light he'd been blinded for hours. But why lock him in this bejeweled cell? Would the drink poison him? Would the food burn through his tongue and throat?

One wall dissolved into a shower of frost, and Domnall ran toward it only to be hurled back across the chamber. He shoved himself to his feet as Prince Iolar entered in a flurry of snowflakes. The leader of the demons glowed as white-gold as his wings before he folded them away. Domnall looked down to see the prince dragging after him a small, limp body. It was a woman, her garments sodden and filthy with gray mud and huge swaths of scarlet.

"On your knees in his presence," the big Sluath that came in after Iolar bellowed.

Domnall smiled and uttered again the only two words he'd said to the demons since being dragged into this place.

"Fack ye."

The prince chuckled. "Still defiant, even when coddled. You see, Danar? I was right."

"As ever, my prince." The bigger demon ducked his head.

"I bring a gift, Hunter." He hoisted the

unconscious female to her feet and clutched
her chin, turning her slack face from side to
side. "Rather disheveled at present, but she
should clean up well. I neglected to ask her
name when I took her. No matter, I'll etch her
with yours." He turned her, and ripped open
the back of her strange tunic.

"No," Domnall shouted, and then tried
again in a more moderate tone. "'Tis no need
to mark her."

"She's our property." The Sluath's claws
began to glow with a black light before he
dragged them along the woman's spine,
etching glyphs into her skin. "You needn't
think of her as a being. She's more a toy."

Danar licked his lips, watching the
torment.

Iolar finished the marking. "There.
Consider her yours until we return from the
next culling."

Domnall stared at him. "I dinnae want a
female."

"A pity. You might have mentioned that
you prefer males. Or perhaps I might have
guessed it from the company you kept." The
prince turned her to face him and took hold

of her neck, squeezing. "I'll dispatch this one and fetch something more to your taste. Do you prefer them older, younger, or perhaps…" He smirked. "…very, very young?"

Domnall rushed over and snatched the woman away from him, tucking her against him. Beads of blood from the marks the Sluath had made spread warm wet spots on his arms.

"Return the lass to her tribe, and I'll no' fight ye or yers again."

"Lying to me is foolish. I'll always know when you do." The demon smiled. "But I find it encouraging that you would try. The endless litany of 'fack ye' has become so boring. Enjoy yourself."

Iolar and his guard retreated through the wall, which solidified into stone. Domnall felt two small hands grip his tunic, and looked down into the captive's mud-smeared face. Her eyes, more beautiful than the sapphires and amethysts studding the walls, shifted quickly as she found her footing.

"Are you one of those things?" she asked, her voice low but steady.

She'd been pretending to be unconscious,

Domnall realized, even through the pain of
being marked.

"No, lass. I'm a prisoner, like ye." Carefully he released her and stepped back so she
could see what had been done to him. "I'm
Domnall mag Raith, a Pritani hunter."

She reached out to touch the claw marks
on his arm, and nodded as she met his gaze
again. "Jenna Cameron. I was…I am an
architect." She took in a deep breath. "Domnall, how do we get out of here?"

⚜

JENNA LISTENED to every word as though she
were hearing the tale of someone else's life.

"I cannae recall more than that," Domnall
admitted after recounting his memory of their
first meeting. "Taking you and putting you at
my mercy… They wished me to use you.
Another of their torments."

He sounded almost ashamed, but she
knew he wasn't that kind of man.

"If you wanted to violate a helpless
woman, you could have done that in the ash
grove." She took hold of his hands. "You

didn't then, so I'm sure you didn't when we were Sluath slaves."

He nodded. "How could we escape, then, thirteen centuries apart?"

"Maybe the same way they took us from different times." Jenna frowned at the water rapidly rising over her bare feet. "I think the drains in here might be clogged."

Domnall turned his head, and then strode over to where the cascade had been channeled through the wall.

"No, *luaidh*. They've been closed off."

Stone grated, and the sound of the falling water swelled to a roar as another waterfall appeared beside the first. Jenna looked up at the new opening in the ceiling, and then turned around to see a stone panel descending in front of the stairs.

Domnall's body blurred as he rushed to it. He moved impossibly fast, and gripped the edge of the panel, straining to keep it up. Jenna slogged through the rising water to help him, but by then blood had begun running through his fingers. With a bellow of pain, he snatched his hands back and the panel slammed down to seal off the chamber. He threw his shoulder at it, trying to dislodge the stone, but it remained in place.

Glancing down at the water, which was now lapping at their knees, Jenna performed some quick mental calculations. "We've got about ten minutes to get those drains open before we run out of air. Can you drown?"

"I've never tried to." Domnall went to the nearest channel from the pool and knelt down in the water, reaching under it. "The ducts are blocked by stone. 'Twillnae move."

"The gates in the ceiling are too high to reach, even if you could hold me on your shoulders." She felt as frustrated as she had in the cider house, and then pressed a wet hand to her brow as she recalled how she had gotten out of it, twice. "I forgot to show you my trick. I wonder if it works with stone as well as wood."

Domnall caught her as she started toward the stone panel. "You cannae move it, lass."

"I'm not planning to." Aware that something could still go terribly wrong, she reached up and kissed him. "If I don't make it, float up to the top and try to close the gates. That may release the stones sealing the ducts."

"What do you mean to try?" He waded over to the panel with her. "Jenna."

She smiled up at him. "I'm glad they brought me to you, Domnall."

Taking a deep breath, she placed her hand on the stone panel. Summoning her power took even less time than the last attempt, and the transition to ghost-form happened almost instantly. Carefully she pushed her fingers into the panel, waiting for pain but feeling only heat on her skin. Quickly she moved through it, emerging on the other side by the stairs.

A muffled shout of her name came from the other side of the panel.

"I'm all right," she called back once she'd solidified, and then rushed up the steps.

As she'd suspected the door leading to the outer passage had closed, and now appeared like a solid stone wall on the inside. She shifted and pushed herself through it, taking on her corporeal form on the other side. She tripped over something, and saw the stone Domnall had used to wedge the door open now lay a foot from where it had been.

Her clothes steamed, and dry hair fell in her face. Passing through stone had evidently created more intense friction than doing the same through wood, but her drenched garments and hair had given her some protection. Filing that away for future reference, Jenna turned and pressed the wall stones.

"Come on," she muttered. "Let him out of there."

The entry opened, and from below came the sound of churning water. She hurried back down, stopping halfway to see Domnall at the bottom of the steps. Incredibly the bathing chamber behind him had emptied, and the second fall had disappeared. Along with the water, all the color had drained from his face.

"I know I should have told you about this," Jenna said quickly. "I didn't think you'd believe me. The first time I did it at the cider house, I thought I was going crazy. Until I did it again."

He stood watching her for another long moment before he blurred, and suddenly he was only an inch away from her.

"You haven't explained how you can move that fast," she pointed out, hoping to add that to her defense. "You're like a giant hummingbird."

"'Tis a power you possessed in your time, to become as a wraith?" he demanded.

"No. I've only been able to do it since I woke up here." Jenna tried to smile. "It did save us from drowning, so it's a good surprise, right?"

Domnall yanked her into his arms and tossed her over his shoulder. He carried her up to the steps and into the passage, and kicked the wall door back into place. Only then did he put her down and look all over her.

"You're so hot."

"Yes." She pressed her lips together until she was almost sure she wouldn't laugh. "That's, ah, a nice compliment in my time."

"I dinnae speak of your beauty." He set her at arm's length. "Doing thus, becoming a wraith, it heats you." He ran his palm over her shoulder, her cheek, and then her hair. "You feel as if you've stood too close to a hearth for a long while."

"It happens after I move through something." In simple terms she explained how friction worked. "Wood isn't as dense as stone, so leaving the cider house didn't create as much heat. Being wet helped, I think."

His eyes narrowed. "To walk through stone too often, you reckon 'twould set fire to you?"

"I'm not sure. I certainly don't plan to find out." She glanced back at the wall. "What I do know is that chamber isn't a well or a bath house."

Domnall's jaw tightened. "'Tis a drowning trap, meant to kill whoever entered the chamber. Yet it didnae seal until after we loved."

"I found the passage door closed and tripped over the wedge stone when I came through it," Jenna told him, suddenly aware of what that meant. "Closing the door must be what triggers the room to seal. But maybe the door was too heavy for the stone."

He bent down and picked up the stone, weighing it in his hand. "Or someone who wishes us dead came and moved it."

Chapter Twenty-Four

By midday Galan had come to appreciate the endurance of his hired men. They rode swiftly and silently, stopping only when signaled by their leader to rest and water their horses. Without his prompting two stood watch while the others passed a jug and shared the food they'd brought. Most said nothing but watched him closely.

"Never mind the lads," the scarred-faced leader told Galan as he offered him the jug. "You fash them, Stranger. You come alone to us, yet you've enough gold to buy an army. 'Tis the kind of treasure that might make the owner a plump target."

Galan met his shrewd gaze. "Do you reckon I'm worried?"

The other man corked the jug. "You neednae fear for your own throat. We ken you'd leave behind the gold you promised us." The leader chuckled. "You're an odd one, Brother." With a sharp yell, he summoned his men to mount their horses.

It took the rest of the afternoon to navigate their way through the rocky slopes and passes to reach Wachvale. As the only village within a day's ride of the battle site, the mercenary leader had assured Galan that his quarry would have stopped there to rest and barter. Galan expected that the curious villagers would have watched the Mag Raith depart, and perhaps have gleaned some idea of where the hunters intended to go.

At first sight of the cottages the mercenaries fell into two ranks, each spreading out on either side of Galan and their leader. Two young men carrying cudgels appeared on either side of the rutted cart trail leading into the center of the village. They took in the mercenaries for a moment, and then turned and ran shouting.

Galan peered at the narrow pass on the other side of the village, but all he spotted was a pasture filled with sheep. "What lay over there?"

"Grass," the mercenary leader said, sounding bored. "Naught more from here to the midlands."

Galan grunted and watched as the village's headman approached them, his weathered face wary and gleaming with fresh perspiration. One of the mercenaries drew his sword, and trotted forward, ready to strike.

"We've naught to trade until after harvest," the headman told them, his eyes darting along the lines of the mounted men. "Ye're welcome to water your horses, but then ye must ride on."

"Naught to trade? Surely no'." The mercenary leader made a show of inspecting the village. "I see stock and tools. Your swine pens look full. I reckon you've even a few comely wenches cowering in those hovels."

The headman swallowed hard and his face paled. "Naught until after harvest."

"We come seeking five hunters and a female," Galan said flatly. "They'd be traveling

light and swift. The men call themselves
Mag Raith."

The headman scowled. "Then ye've come
on a fool's chase after the long-dead, stranger."
He made a circling gesture over his chest.
"Begone with ye."

"We'll speak to your people first," the
mercenary leader told him. "Summon them to
the green, now."

Folding his arms to hide his shaking hands,
the headman spat on the ground.

At a signal from the leader, the sword-
wielding mercenary shot forward, slashing his
blade. A moment later the defiant man's head
tumbled to the ground, followed by his body.
As screams came from the cottages the
remaining mercenaries followed the first,
chasing every villager they saw. Their blades
ran red with blood as they hacked and skewered away.

"I need to question them," Galan told the
leader, who sat watching the carnage with a
faint sneer.

"You'll have your chance, after we've had
ours. If any survive."

The leader rode after his men, shouting for them to drag out the females.

As the senseless violence went on, Galan considered trying to stop it. But riding into the fray meant courting injury or even death at the hands of his own hirelings. The villagers likely knew nothing, but whatever they had seen of the Mag Raith would go with them to their graves.

One of the cudgel-wielding young men also held a torch and tried to strike a mercenary with it. But the mounted man snatched it from his grip before he beheaded him. The torch went flying onto one of the thatched roofs, setting it alight and driving out those hiding inside. Inspired by this, the rest of the mercenaries began setting fire to the other hovels.

It was time he left them to it, Galan decided, completely disgusted now. Yet as he turned his mount away from the killing a brute rode around him to block his escape.

"You'll no' leave until we're done," the mercenary said, grinning through the blood spattered on his face as he lifted his sword. "Then you'll take us to our gold, and what more you've hidden." He jabbed toward the village. "Ride in, then."

Galan turned his mount around and urged him forward, guiding the nervous horse around the corpses already littering the green. Deliberately he stopped before a burning cottage, dismounting and taking the Sluath's feather from his belt. He held it up, releasing it on a gust of smoky wind, and watched it land in the flames.

"Here's one for you, Stranger."

The leader dragged an older woman along, dropping her to collapse at Galan's feet before riding off after a younger female. The crone covered her head with her arms and wailed.

Galan reached down, taking her by the arm and hoisting her upright. Soot stained her face and crooked nose.

"I seek five hunters and a wench, traveling by mount," he told her, but he had to shake her to get her attention. "The hunters are strong and say little. The lass, she's young, with dark hair and eyes like gems." The woman uttered a shrill sound and struggled against his grasp. "Did any strangers stop here in the last twoday, or ride past? Ken you the direction they took?" He drew his dagger and held it to her throat. "Answer, and I'll spare you."

"No, ye willnae." Tears made tracks through the filth on her cheeks. "Be ye forever cursed for what ye've done this day."

"I've done naught, Crone." He leaned closer. "But a word from me, and the others shall see to it you ken suffering beyond all imagining. You'll beg them to end you. *Tell me.*"

Suddenly she calmed, and nodded as if at last she understood him. But as her gaze shifted past him, her eyes widened. Without another word she surged forward, cutting her own throat on his dagger.

Galan dropped her and turned to see glittering light filling the narrow pass on the other side of the village. From it strode Prince Iolar, his gleaming wings spread wide. Without a cloud in the sky, the Sluath had ridden no storm. Had Galan summoned him from an underworld gateway, as the legends told?

Huge flurries of ice and snow billowed out from Iolar's gilded feathers. All of the mercenaries stopped where they stood, their mouths agape and their swords lowering. Snowflakes whitened their shoulders and heads as the Sluath landed, and the flames of the burning cottages slowly died. Frost raced across the blood-soaked green, creeping up the legs of the brutes who tried to run, freezing them in place.

"Ah." The Sluath's golden eyes searched the mercenaries' faces. "So many to harvest."

When the prince reached the one nearest him, he plunged his hand into the man's chest. Power surged into the helpless mortal before Iolar wrenched from him a heart formed of black mist. Unhinging his jaw until it dropped down to his chest, the prince stuffed the ghastly apparition into his mouth and devoured it whole.

The victim toppled backward, his dead eyes filling with snow.

One by one the other mercenaries shared the same fate, until the prince reached the leader of the brutes. The mortal fell to his knees, begging for mercy. His voice died as Iolar shoved his claws into his face and pulled from it a pulsing sphere of blood-colored mist.

The leader's body collapsed as the prince tucked the strange orb under his wing.

Galan stood his ground as the Sluath approached him, revolted and yet fascinated by the demon's gruesome feasting. It seemed all the old legends about the demons devouring mortal souls had been true. Yet the sphere he'd taken from the last brute seemed something else.

When Iolar stopped before him he quickly bowed. "The hired men turned on me in the end. My thanks for your aid, my prince."

The Sluath's wings bristled, showering cutting ice crystals over him. "Do you think I came to rescue you from your own idiocy? Had you not provided me with such tempting morsels, you fool, I'd have swallowed your soul."

He'd have to offer Iolar something more to satisfy his fiendish appetite.

"'Twas folly to put my trust in these wicked mortals," Galan said evenly. "Yet I did learn something. The Mag Raith werenae seen by the villagers. I reckon they rode through the night to cross the valley."

Iolar glanced around at the dead and

wounded. "Why would they need to hide their passage?"

"They strive to elude your wrath, my prince. They willnae have gone far, for the horses and the wench shall need rest." He made a sweeping gesture. "They'd seek shelter near here, mayhap within five leagues."

"You're not keeping your part of our bargain, Aedth." Although he sounded annoyed, Iolar's gaze moved to the horizon. "Still, I smell a coming storm. I shall send my scouts when it arrives."

"I shall ride west to the midlands," Galan promised.

He waited until the prince stalked across the green toward the pass before he wiped the melting ice from his face. His hand came away stained a watery red and flecked with soot. It reminded him of the tears winding down the crone's filthy face, and what she had said.

Be ye forever cursed for what ye've done this day.

Chapter Twenty-Five

When they emerged from the castle Domnall summoned the men with a whistle, and asked them to join him around the fire. Each one now wore one of the tartans they had traded for, and to see them garbed like proper Scotsmen made him feel a little odd. They were Pritani, and yet the tribes were no more.

"We saved one for you," Mael said and tossed a red and black plaid to him.

"My thanks," Domnall replied but draped it around Jenna's shoulders. "We've much to tell you, brothers."

The tracker grinned broadly. "Aye, but 'tis already written on your faces. We wish you both joy in each other."

"It's not about that," Jenna said, her tone somber. "Domnall told me everything about what's happened to you five, but..." She paused and glanced at him. "I think for it all to make sense I'd better start with what happened to me in my time."

Domnall sat beside his lover as she told the Mag Raith of her life in the distant future, and the grim fashion in which it had ended. He noted that she used simple words to describe her strange world, but even so the men fell silent and watched her with open astonishment.

"I was alone, helpless and dying when the Sluath appeared. It seems like that part of the Pritani legends is true. Since I was transported back seven centuries, it's also obvious that they can travel through time." Her lips twisted. "What we think happened next is what came back to Domnall."

Mael drew back a little, his expression alarmed. "'Tis more?"

Domnall nodded, and then recounted his recollection of his lavish prison, and Jenna being brought to him and marked by the Sluath. He also described the drowning trap beneath the ruins, and how Jenna had escaped and freed him. When he finished speaking the only sound for a time came from wood cracking in the flames.

Edane uttered a chuckle, and then grimaced. "Forgive me. 'Tis only I've long wondered how you twice escaped the cider house. 'Tis no' so surprising, I reckon. During the battle with the Sluath we—"

"That 'twill keep, Archer." Broden leaned forward, his eyes intent on Jenna. "You ken why the facking *skeg* brought you to the chieftain, dinnae you?"

"I was some kind of twisted gift." She reached for Domnall's hand, twining her fingers through his. "I know he'd never force himself on me. What I think we did was find a way to escape them. Somehow in the process we got separated in time."

"And the rest of the Mag Raith, then?" Kiaran asked, his voice tight. "What became of us?"

"'Twould seem they separated us from Domnall and the lass," Mael said, frowning at the falconer. "He didnae leave us behind with the demons, or you shouldnae be here to ask."

Kiaran rose to his feet and came around the fire to crouch beside Jenna, his expression intent. "Ken you anything more of the Mag Raith in the underworld? Why the demons took us? Did the facking prince say?"

"I didn't remember meeting Domnall. That's his memory. I just know I would have been safe with him." She reached out and touched the falconer's arm. "Has anything come back to you?"

He ducked his head. "No' a moment of it. I've tried to recall it every day since we awoke, but 'tis lost to me."

Domnall heard the shame in his tone, and reached over to grip his shoulder. "I remembered but a few minutes with Jenna and the demon, yet that proves our memories werenae destroyed. Our past 'twill come back to us."

Kiaran rubbed a hand over his face before he nodded.

"Aye, and mayhap this place shall unveil more," Edane said, eyeing the outer wall.

"Tomorrow we should begin a thorough search of the ruins," Jenna told him. "We've already found one intact sublevel–"

"No," Domnall said. "'Tis too dangerous,

as we both ken." He looked around at his men. "We'll pack up tonight, and ride out at dawn. They'll no' welcome us back at the village, but we can reach the outer midlands in twoday."

Jenna drew her hand from his. "If we go now, we may never find out what happened to us. I got my life back today. Besides, how dangerous can it be when the five of you…" Her voice trailed off. "Is this because I'm mortal? In case you've forgotten, I saved *you* today."

No Pritani or *dru-wid* female would ever have challenged him so openly, especially under threat. That Jenna would now prodded his temper. They might not have formally mated, but she had given herself to him. It was time she understood what that meant.

"For that I'm grateful," he said softly. "But it doesnae alter the danger here. Someone kicked that wedge aside, and 'twas no' any of mine."

"You don't know that for certain." Jenna scrambled to her feet. "The door could have been too heavy for the stone. Don't tell me you believed that old woman's superstitious nonsense."

"Kiaran, we should check the mounts," Edane said, quickly rising. "And see to the saddles.

Mael also stood and avoided Jenna's gaze. "Broden and I'll sort out the packs, and fill the skins. All shall be made ready."

Domnall waited until the men departed . "Lass, I dinnae discuss my orders. I decide such matters for the good of all."

"Yes, Mael told me all about it, but that's not how it is in my time," Jenna said flatly. "I remember my life now. In the future women don't have to blindly obey men. We're not treated like livestock or property. We make our own decisions."

"Aye." The anger flaring in her eyes made him itch to haul her into his arms and kiss her breathless. "Yet you're no' in your time."

She peered at him. "This isn't about me at all. You don't want to know. You think if you leave now that we'll never remember the rest. What are you so afraid of?" When he didn't reply her expression turned stubborn. "I have to find out what they did."

Her fury fed his own. "You vowed you wouldnae go anywhere without me."

"I'm not going." Pain flickered across her face before she removed his tartan. She put it in his hands before she turned her back on him. "You're leaving me."

Domnall watched her head into the forest, his hands knotting. He should let her walk off her anger, and then speak with her again once he'd regained his calm. The twilight deepened as she disappeared into the trees, and he thought of the last time he'd seen his sire's face.

The scant light of a single flame had shown Domnall what he had done. He remembered how his fingers had shaken when he'd reached for the hilt of his sire's dagger, only to have his hand seized by the headman.

Curse ye for a coward. Ye've killed the tribe.

KIARAN LEFT Edane with the horses and a lie about seeing to his kestrels. He knew all of his birds now perched high in the trees to keep watch over the camp. Through their eyes he

watched Domnall and Jenna argue before the
lass stalked off. A moment later the chieftain
followed, his expression grim.

You've met your match there, Brother.

He felt a pang of sympathy for the big
man, for Domnall had answered to no one but
Galan for the last twelve centuries. Even in
their mortal lives he'd cared little for the
females, preferring the hunt above the pursuit
of a mate. Kiaran had always admired his
staunch indifference to everything, even his
duty to the tribe.

The falconer found a spot near one of the
old walls where he could conceal himself, and
there stood as he thought through all that
Domnall and Jenna had revealed. Both had
endured horrors, that much seemed clear, yet
seemed entirely unshaken by their ordeals.
The lass had even concealed from them her
ability to change into ghost-form.

Kiaran understood why she had kept silent
about her gift. Doubtless Galan would have
used it as evidence of her treacherous nature.
But the Mag Raith were all the protection she
had against the headman in a world of which
she knew nothing. To keep them from turning

against her she'd have to make them believe that she was as she claimed.

Just as the Mag Raith believed that he alone had survived a Viking attack that had slaughtered his entire tribe.

The past had never sat easily on him. Even before becoming a hunter Kiaran had endlessly entreated the Gods to give him such strength, especially when the nightmares gnawed at him.

Let me be like the kestrels, and care for naught but the sky, the chase, and the kill.

Yet he'd never be like the birds or the other hunters.

Among Domnall's tribe Kiaran had been tolerated since he had wandered, battered and dazed and starving, into their settlement. It had taken days for the older women to nurse him out of his shocked stupor. After he came back to himself, and began to speak, they took him to see their headman.

Nectan mag Raith had seemed like a tall and terrible giant to Kiaran, and had done nothing to coddle him.

Ye'll tell me how ye came here, lad, and why. Speak the truth now, or I'll drive ye out.

Stuttering and weeping, he'd told Nectan mag Raith of raiders that had come in the night. How his mother had run with him into the forest and the Vikings had pursued them. He spoke of the last thing he remembered, the smashing clout of a raider's fist and waking in darkness. He told the headman what he'd felt when he'd stumbled back to his village, finding it gutted and burned, and every soul there butchered. He'd found his mother's body, and screaming at what had been done to her, he stumbled away. He ran until he dropped, and then limped when he could no longer run, until he reached the Mag Raith.

It was the truth, of sorts, just not Kiaran's.

The headman's expression remained stern throughout Kiaran's blubbering, and then he slapped him, hard enough to make his ears ring.

Weeping, 'tis for bairns and females. If ye're to join my tribe ye'll act a man. Kneel, and pledge yer loyalty to me now, and I'll see ye made a Mag Raith.

From that night Kiaran had never wept again.

Nectan kept his word, and the tribe had adopted him. The women shared the work of feeding and clothing him, while the men attended to his training. Yet none of the families wished to take him as a son. Instead, Kiaran was expected to toil for them from dawn to dusk, doing whatever they asked of him. He'd been no better than a slave.

But he did the work without complaint, since he didn't deserve to be anyone's son.

Kiaran's boyhood remained dismal until he was deemed old enough to look after himself and live on his own. Even then he was expected to build his own *broch* and hunt for himself, for no family owed him anything. But Kiaran soon discovered that he had no skill with a spear, and had to trade work for food to avoid starvation.

All that changed when he found Dive, the first of his kestrels.

Kiaran had been gathering berries when he saw the flutter of feathers in the bramble patch. The kestrel clutched a small vole in her claws, but her wings had become snagged on the sharp thorns. The little bird's dark eyes had met his, and she'd stilled. He'd freed her as gently as he could, and then placed her on the ground. She'd looked up at him before flying off, only to return a short time later, hovering over him.

Holding out his arm, Kiaran had hardly dared to breathe. When the kestrel landed on his wrist, her claws had stabbed deep into his flesh. But he was so enchanted by her that he hardly felt the wounds.

Dive kept coming to him whenever he gathered berries there, and in time he'd discovered her nest, buried in a hollow tree. He brought voles for her and her four young, and wore a leather gauntlet for her to perch on. Soon Dive began teaching her nestlings how to hunt, and Kiaran began to learn, too.

As his prowess with the birds grew, he knew it would cause trouble for him. Among Pritani tribes falconers were prized and respected but they learned their craft from a sire or a master who chose them. Kiaran had no right to use the kestrels even if he knew how.

Broden had been the first to discover his secret when he'd come upon him using Dive to hunt and sporting a fat brace of hares. Instead of condemning Kiaran, or exposing him to Nectan's wrath, he'd helped him make his first set of jesses. He'd also shown him the clever talent he had for trapping. They became friends of sorts, two outcasts hiding their skills from the tribe, until at last they joined Domnall and the others.

The four men became the brothers Kiaran had always longed for, but still he kept the truth hidden.

He blinked back into the present and looked up to see Dive seemingly floating in the air over him, as vigilant as ever. He held out his arm for her to perch, and then looked into her eyes, seeing himself through them. His face made a pale smear in the deepening shadows as he heard Nectan's voice echoing from the past, the night before that last hunt, demanding he do the one thing impossible for him.

Speak the truth and ye'll die. Hold yer tongue and ye'll live.

Kiaran sent Dive off to her perch. By now he reckoned Domnall would have caught up with the lass to settle the discord between them. As willful as she was lovely, Jenna wouldn't cower before the chieftain. She wouldn't run from him. One of the few advantages to Kiaran being passed around the tribe had been to see many types of mated couples, and how they got along, or didn't. Domnall and his lady might not yet realize it, but they suited each other perfectly.

Kiaran would never have such a woman, but he had his birds and his secrets. He pushed away from the wall. That would have to be enough.

Chapter Twenty-Six

D rawn from his labors by mortal screams, Cul kept watch from the slopes overlooking Wachvale. The stench of blood and death tainted every breath he took, speaking much of what had caused the villagers to shriek.

More hunters had come but these had wished only sport.

While Cul built Dun Chaill he'd permitted the villagers to dwell in peace. Simple folk interested only in themselves, they had never strayed beyond their wall. Over time they'd also provided the valuable service of cleaning up whatever he scattered in their pastures. Seeing them butchered by the druid's men displeased him so much he considered taking the druid once the demons left. The only thing that saved the tree-worshipper was his speedy departure, and the sound of moans coming from the burnt cottages.

The dreadful noise told Cul that some of the villagers yet lived.

Mortals such as these had always been as unforgiving as himself. If they survived their wounds, they would burn with hatred for those responsible. Even after seeing that all of the druid's men lay dead beside their murdered kin, it would not be enough. They would go in search of others to see what the druid had done. They would rally enough to begin searching for him. While they deserved vengeance, a search might lead more of their kind to Dun Chaill.

Cul could not permit that. His castle had to remain inviolate until the day came for the justice he sought.

Once the moon rose and night cloaked the ruined village, Cul slipped down from the slopes. From long habit he kept to the shadows as he approached the charmed gate. The dangling bits of quartz made him sneer with contempt. He tore it open, flinging the crystal-studded barricade into the wall. Stones rumbled as a long gap appeared in the stonework, and the sheep herd it protected bleated and scattered.

"Run away, run away," he muttered, watching them. "For you shall have to fend for yourselves now."

He made his way into the village to first inspect the corpses before he entered a cottage. There by a hearth sat an old man covered in blood and rocking back and forth. In his arms he cradled the body of a bairn that had been nearly hacked in two.

As Cul approached the old mortal's tearful gaze met his, and he stiffened. "*Kithan.*"

"No need to fear, Grandfather," he assured him.

As Cul moved behind him, he curled his hands around the wrinkled neck. He caressed his quivering flesh fondly, enjoying the rare contact, until he felt the warmth of blood seeping from the elder's scalp. The amount, and the too-rapid pulse of the villager's heart, suggested he'd bleed out before dawn.

The old man went still, and then uttered his last word. "Why?"

"I have to be sure," Cul said softly, apologetically.

It took only a quick, hard jerk, and the old man slumped back, his hands falling away from the murdered child. Cul looked down on them both for a moment before he nodded and went to the next cottage.

Chapter Twenty-Seven

~~~

As night crept like shadow cats through the woods, Jenna slowed her pace. The last thing she wanted to do was trip and fall into the stream. Sloshing around in the dark where she couldn't see the rocks would result in injuries she didn't need. She was already hurt enough.

Now that she remembered the rest of her life before coming to this time, it shocked her how little she missed the twenty-first century. After school she'd thrown herself into building her career. It had cost her the only two men she'd ever bothered to date. Both had wanted more than an occasional dinner out and casual sex from her. Neither had stirred Jenna's heart, so she'd broken it off each time.

She'd been so focused that she'd had no real friends or interests outside of work.

But the one thing Jenna did miss was being in charge of her life, making her own decisions, and charting her own course. Apparently medieval women didn't get those options.

Domnall could be forgiven for his thirteenth-century attitudes. He probably did believe he was protecting her by overruling her desire to stay and search the ruins. What she couldn't stand was her suspicion that behind all that medieval chauvinism he was hiding something else.

He still doesn't trust me.

The sound of the stream guided her out of the forest, and she made her way carefully down to the soft, short grass that carpeted the bank. Above her the stars had begun buttoning the sky with diamond light. Just above the far ridges she could make out the curved tooth of the rising crescent moon. It made her think of all the nights she'd spent in the office, putting in overtime on some project or another. All that time and effort to show her boss that she was serious about her work, when she could have been sitting by a stream and watching the stars.

It's nothing personal, Hal Maxwell had said, right before he'd had a building blown up on top of her.

Tingling warmth stroked up her spine, but Jenna ignored it as she went to sit on a large flat-topped rock. There was just enough space for her to tuck her legs to one side and brace herself with a hand. When Domnall came up behind her she could feel him like a caress moving from her waist to her shoulders.

Whatever he said now didn't matter. If he intended to force her to leave, she'd find her way back again. Everything she needed to know was right here, waiting to be found.

"You asked what I feared, and I shall tell you." He sat down on the grass beside the rock, and looked out over the slopes. "I didnae plan to return after our last hunt. Before we left the settlement, I killed my sire."

She frowned and turned her head, flinching when she saw how remote his expression had become. He wasn't joking. He'd murdered his father.

"Nectan came to me in the night, while I

slept. I woke as he made to stab me." He joined his hands and rested his forearms on his knees. "We struggled, and I turned the blade on him. Before he could stop me, I drove it into his heart."

"Oh, Domnall, no," Jenna said and shuddered. "Why did he attack you?"

He shook his head. "With his last breath he cursed me. He said I'd killed the tribe. That I'd be forever damned as a coward for it. Then he died."

"You're not a coward." She scrambled down from the rock, and knelt before him. "You didn't do anything wrong. My God, he attacked you while you were sleeping."

"Aye, but I'd taken the life of a headman. 'Twas no greater crime among the Pritani. For years the tribe saw how my sire and I despised each other. His end meant I'd take his place. If I'd confessed to killing him, they'd have put me to death by ritual sacrifice. I wished to live." He regarded her. "Thus, I hid my sire's body, gathered my hunters at dawn, and left."

She put her arms around him, feeling him stiffen before he pulled her close.

"'Twas why the Sluath took us, I reckon. My wickedness and my cowardice drew them to me." He buried his face in her hair for a moment. "You cannae count how many times I've wished I hadn't fought him. That I'd let him end me. For what I did I deserve to suffer, but the others wouldnae be damned but for my evil."

Jenna drew back and cradled his face with her hands. "Did you want him dead? Is that really why you stabbed him?"

Domnall shook his head. "I didnae even ken 'twas my sire until he spoke his last. 'Twas too dark to see his face."

"Then you did nothing wrong. You defended yourself." When he averted his gaze, she made him look at her. "You fought for your life. How could that be evil?"

He closed his eyes, and touched his brow to hers. "It tore at my heart to see what I'd done. Truly I'd forever despised him for how hard and cruel he'd been to me. Yet I never once wished him dead. I but wanted him to care for me, even as I saw he never would."

"You saved yourself. You saved me. You even spared Galan after he tried to shoot me."

She brushed her lips over his. "You're not a killer, Domnall."

His shoulders shook, and he uttered a low sound as he lifted her onto his lap. "I wish to take you far from here. To build a home for us, where we might abide in peace." His mouth thinned. "Yet too I think the Sluath shall hunt us forever."

"We escaped them twice," Jenna said and curled her arms around his neck as she considered how difficult it must have been for him to tell her about his father. She needed to do something in return. "I want to stay at Dun Chaill, but it's not as important to me as being with you. If you really think we're in danger, I'll leave with you tomorrow."

"Thank the Gods." Domnall drew her down with him, turning on his side so they lay facing each other in the cool, soft grass. "If we love again, more memories may return to us." He said that with a trace of self-mockery.

She pressed against him, and trailed her fingertips over the ink on his arm. "Or we could just make love because we want to. I think we should."

"I delight in how you think."

Domnall spanned her jaw with his hand, and covered her mouth with his.

All the kisses before this one had been frantic and passionate, but now they tasted each other slowly. Jenna caught his breath and gave him hers in soft, endless sighs. Desire began building between them, hardening Domnall's muscles and softening her own. His big, tough body made her feel so deliciously feminine and delicate. When he rolled her onto her back, the weight of him between her thighs felt so good she never wanted to move again.

He drew her arms over her head, and stripped off her tunic. His head lowered as he nuzzled her bare breasts, kissing and nipping at her puckered nipples. The smell of him rolled over her, dusky and deep with masculine arousal. She could feel the ridge of his erection against her pussy, pulsing now with his need. Excitement streaked through her, bowing her back and urging her thighs up to cradle his hips.

"You're making me hot again," Jenna murmured, caressing his hard chest with her palms. "And this time I'm not walking through walls."

He faked a scowl. "You drove the wits from me when you vanished into the stone." He sat back to tug off her trousers, and then went still as he gazed down at her. "Gods, but surely you're the loveliest thing I've ever beheld."

"Now you're driving me out of my wits." Jenna reached up for him, and then gasped as he shifted down and spread her thighs. "Domnall, what are you…ah."

The feel of his mouth on her pussy made a low cry burst from her, and then Jenna became awash with aching need. He kissed and licked her with hungry fervor, his tongue stroking her and teasing her until she gripped the grass beside her and jerked her hips. His hands slid under her, holding her where he wanted her, and then he began laving her clit without stopping. The persistent wet, firm loving of his tongue sent her thrashing as she came apart, shaking helplessly from the intensity of the climax.

Domnall kissed and blew his breath on her throbbing nub, lifting his damp mouth at last as he surged up over her. She tore at his laces, needing him inside her so much she couldn't speak or think or breathe.

"Ken how sweet you are," he crooned before he kissed her, sharing the slickness from her sex on his tongue.

Tasting herself in his mouth made Jenna want to shove him over and take him in hers, but he had freed his heavy cock by then, and notched the satiny head between her folds. Her thighs quivered as he began to press in, sinking into the honeyed wetness he'd created, his body tensing over hers.

No memories came back to Jenna this time, which gave her the chance to savor every inch he sank into her. Feeling his body merge with hers gave her a sense of being completed. She didn't need anything more than him coming into her, taking her, claiming her. If he'd left Dun Chaill she wouldn't have stayed behind, she realized. She'd have ridden after him, unable to bear being apart from the man she...

"I love you," she breathed. Something inside her that had been closed off and locked and guarded suddenly flooded out of her with the words. "I loved you when we were slaves. I loved you when I woke up in the ash grove. I just couldn't let myself feel it."

"Yet now you do." Domnall's eyes shifted as he looked all over her face, and his mouth curved with fierce satisfaction. "Aye, 'tis everywhere on you, this love for me. We'll wed as soon as we may."

He wasn't asking, Jenna thought, but it thrilled her to know he wanted her that much. "Yes."

Domnall drew out of her, and then surged back inside. "We'll never be parted again, *luaidh*."

As a mortal she couldn't promise that, but for tonight she'd let him believe it. "No, my love. Not ever. Oh." He pumped so deep she felt it in her breasts, and released a shivery moan.

He bent his head to catch the sound, gripping her bottom with one big hand. Then he fucked her, so slowly she writhed under him, desperate and delighted, loving and needing.

Their bodies moved together as if they'd been lovers all their lives. Domnall knew exactly how to touch her, his fingers stroking her mound and the curve of her bottom with sensual relish. She could feel him swelling against the clasp of her softness, eager and hard. With the deep shockwaves gathering in her core it wouldn't be long before they both came for each other, but he was still trying to be gentle.

"I love how you fack me," Jenna told him, using his word for it. His eyes narrowed and glittered as he plowed deeper into her. "That's what I want, yes. Give me everything. I need it. I need all of you." She kissed his shoulder. "Be my husband, Domnall."

He muttered something under his breath, sweat dripping from his face, and then his body blurred.

Jenna shrieked with astonished joy, feeling his cock stroking in and out of her impossibly fast. Her bliss broke over her a moment before he roared and plunged one last time, fucking her with his seed and his quicksilver shaft.

Domnall almost collapsed on her before he rolled over, keeping their bodies joined as he held her atop him. "You bewitch my sense from me, *luaidh*. I might have harmed you."

She couldn't move, but she managed a

shake of her head. "That was…" There wasn't a word in her vocabulary to describe it, so instead she made a sexy sound.

"You'll truly wed me?" The hesitance in his voice made her look at him. "'Twas meant to be asked, no' demanded."

Gods, he was stealing her heart all over again. "We can have a ceremony or whatever your people do, but I feel like we're married already. Except…" Domnall's green eyes watched her intently. "What does *luaidh* mean?"

He grinned, wrapped his arms around her, and kissed the top of her head. "Loved one."

Chapter Twenty-Eight

After making love much of the night, Domnall woke near dawn feeling a pervasive, curious contentment. He'd never slept after the sun rose, but he'd never loved sitting alone by the fire before it did. Now he would never have to again, at least for Jenna's lifetime.

He glanced down at his lover, who lay sprawled over him in complete abandon under his tartan. Dew had spangled her dark locks and even her eyelashes, and the sunrise bathed her with its pale golden light. She smelled of loving, and him, the most intimate fragrance of all. In that moment he could have easily vowed to never leave the spot.

"Why are you watching me sleep?" she murmured without opening her eyes.

"Because if I wake you, we must leave this place to ride all day." She would always be a bit cross in the early hours, he thought, because she slept so soundly. "I thought to spare you as long as I may, as you're a female, and unused to it." The glare she gave him after she lifted her head made him chuckle. "You see? Now we must dress and return to the camp."

"I've changed my mind. I don't love you anymore."

She pushed herself off him and staggered to her feet, naked and yawning. As he dressed Domnall watched her wriggle into her trews, admiring the sweet curves and lovely smoothness of her torso. She would be his now, for as long as she lived. He would enjoy every day of her life, every hour, every moment. Yet when she turned around to look for her tunic, a flash of silver made him reach for her.

"Oh, no, sir," Jenna said, quickly skittering away. "Not if I'm going to be in the saddle all day."

"'Tis no' that." He gently turned her until

he could see clearly the length of her spine. Carefully he touched the altered glyphs. "The Sluath's skinwork, 'tis no longer black. 'Tis turned to silver."

"Okay." She tried to look over her shoulder, and then frowned at him. "Did you notice? So is yours."

Domnall lifted his arm into the sunlight, which made the new, paler color of his ink glow. "'Tis been unchanged since I awoke in the grove." He glanced at the ground where they had slept. "What the fack did this?"

"Maybe our facking," she said wryly, and then took a closer look at his arm. "Domnall, the ink didn't change color. It looks like it's fading."

He watched the play of emotions on her face. "What do you reckon?"

"You told me about your father last night, and I agreed to leave Dun Chaill. Then we made love and agreed to be married." She smiled a little. "According to your legends the Sluath prey on people who are helpless and alone. That's not either of us anymore."

He took hold of her hands. "And we'll

never be from this day forth, *luaidh*. I promise you."

"If we're married, or going to be married, we should make some official vows." She pretended to think for a moment. "I promise not to argue with you in front of the men. I'll wait until we're alone."

He nodded. "I vow no' to beat you." When she laughed, he frowned. "Dinnae tell me men in your time yet do."

"They don't, unless they want to go to jail, but thank you. I would appreciate not being beaten." She tapped a finger against her chin. "I promise not to get mad at you unless you really make me angry."

"I pledge to kiss you as often as I may, but not as I wish." He tipped up her chin. "For I'd never cease kissing you."

He kissed her then and when their mouths parted Jenna's eyes lit up with happiness. "Can we negotiate on that one?"

When they arrived at the camp, they found the hunters gathering and packing the last of their belongings, saddling the mounts and extinguishing the fire's embers.

"Fair morning," Mael hailed them. "Lass, do I saddle five or six mounts?"

"Six," Jenna called back, making him grin. She said to Domnall in a lower voice, "I need to go water a tree. Give me five minutes?"

He nodded, and watched her hurry off before he went to check the tack on her horse. He knew the tracker was watching him as well, and said, "Ask."

"I but wish to ken how you persuaded that obstinate little thing to come with us," Mael said. "Did you ply her with whisky? Threaten to tie her to a mount? Drop on your knees and beg?"

"I drove her near crazed with pleasure, again and again." As the other man gaped at him, he chuckled. "Only she agreed to come with us before I did. I cannae claim it my coaxing. In all things, she chooses to do as she will."

From his expression Mael was even more perplexed. "Well, then." The tracker seemed lost for words but then he shrugged. "Jolly good for the lass."

As he led his mount away, Kiaran cocked his head at Mael's back and Domnall frowned.

Jolly?

What had got into the man?

Domnall's gaze shifted to the nearest wall of the ruins, and his unease grew.

ONCE SHE'D DEALT with nature's call Jenna walked back along Dun Chaill's outer wall. It still puzzled her that the stonework that had collapsed didn't appear to fit in the gaping spaces they'd left. Squatters or salvagers may have moved or stolen some of the loose stones, but it seemed unlikely. Transporting such heavy objects would have required a lot of muscle and horse power.

As she reached toward one of the gaps to test the stones, she tripped.

After coming to a stumbling stop, and barely managing to stay upright, she looked back to see that her boot had caught on a gnarled and knobby root. She had to laugh a little. After everything she'd been through, to have tripped and hit her head on the wall, would have been irony in the extreme.

She glanced back along her path to give

the ruins a final look. She'd always loved reading about old medieval castles, and how well so many had weathered the passage of time. Their deceptively simple construction often survived for centuries beyond more modern buildings.

Domnall may have hated Dun Chaill, but she loved it.

As she sighed a little and turned to go, something near the root caught her eye. A sparkling, light green stone peeked at her.

"What's this?" she muttered, as she reached down to pry it out of the dirt.

But it was much bigger than she'd imagined: an eight-sided crystal the size of her fist. Brushing away the soil from the facets revealed its lovely color, like an emerald filled with mist.

Jenna glanced around, trying to see from where it might have come. Another glitter closer to a gap in the wall caught her eye. She went over and retrieved a slightly smaller crystal, this time the rich red color of a garnet.

"Not-so-buried treasure." She saw more glittering gems inside the wall, forming a somewhat uneven line into the interior. "Or maybe breadcrumbs."

At the very least they could be used to trade for supplies along the journey to the midlands. So Dun Chaill was offering up a final treasure. She smiled to herself and picked up the next few shining stones. But as she moved through the roofless passages, she stopped picking up the gems. If she went too far inside, she realized, she might need them to quickly find her way back out.

"And if I can't, I'll just walk through the walls," Jenna promised herself.

Light shifted over her as her footsteps stopped crunching the dead leaves lining the passage. She'd reached another bed of fern, which completely covered the ground and hid any other gems that might have been dropped. Had the castle's builders been forced out by some catastrophe? Had they run with their arms filled with their precious things, dropping them in their haste? It couldn't have been a fire. There wasn't a single scorch mark on any of the interior stones. The floors would have been thick with soot and burnt wood after a blaze.

It hadn't suddenly collapsed, either. She knew only too well what that kind of disaster looked like.

Jenna stopped on the threshold of a large, wide room. The space, punctuated by tall trees that provided a kind of roof, looked to be some kind of central gathering area. Probably a great hall, she recalled from the books she'd read. It would be where the resident lord would conduct his business, hold banquets and parties, and even meet with important visitors.

Not a stick of furniture remained, but she could make out some faded paintings on the remains of the lime-washed walls. Swirls of yellow and red, dotted by five-petalled flowers, curled like giant, ghostly vines around the room. Something about it made her imagine the castle literally growing out of the original fortress, spreading like a wild garden of stone. It also brought a twinge of discomfort as she saw all the passages leading off to other parts of the ruins. One in particular had a huge crystal dropped just in front of the open arch.

All right. I'll play your little game. Just one more room.

She crossed to it and stood peering inside.

It was too dark to see anything from here. She'd just go inside and take one peek. If it was a treasure room, and the lord of the castle hadn't taken everything, it could help them build that home Domnall wanted for them. If there were more gems like the ones she'd seen, it might even build them their own castle.

She heard a faint sound as she stepped inside, like the snap of a dry twig, and paused to make sure of her footing.

The interior beyond the arch appeared completely dark except for a single, narrow sun beam that had found its way down through the tree canopy. Nothing it touched sparkled, but Jenna saw what looked like long rows of full-body armor. On the walls she could see the silhouettes of spears, swords, shields and other weapons. The smell of something like oil and moss grew heavy in the air. She moved inside, being careful to look down before she took a step, and finally made it to the center of the chamber.

"Oh, boy." She turned around slowly to take it all in.

Dozens of life-size statues cast in iron surrounded her. Splotches of moss covered the top of their heads like green curly toupees, but otherwise they seemed untouched by time. All appeared to be men dressed in primitive-looking garments. Whoever had made them had fashioned each one with unique features and clothing without any duplication. Some wore furs so finely detailed they resembled real pelts, as if someone had skinned animals made of iron. All of the statues carried swords and daggers that looked incredibly sharp too.

"No more gems except you guys." Though the precious stones had been nice, now her heart started to race. This might be the clue they needed to understand what had happened to the old fortress. She had to get Domnall. "Be right back."

On her way out she heard a metallic, scraping sound and glanced back to see the sunlight expanding. As the beam touched each statue the eyes seemed to blink and then glare at her. She almost laughed at herself, until the statue in the center of the chamber slowly lifted its arm to brandish its sword. The sight astounded her so much she couldn't move. Then all the statues started to raise their weapons as if they meant to attack her.

The small snapping sound she'd heard when she entered the chamber hadn't come from her.

It was a tripwire.

Keeping her eyes on them, Jenna snatched the small dirk from her boot and held the blade up the way Domnall had showed her. Carefully she took one step back, and then another. Whatever was in this chamber wasn't worth getting hacked at by an army of medieval automatons.

"Sorry," she told the glaring statues. "I didn't mean to turn you on."

Something whizzed from the midst of their pack and clanged against her blade with a bright spark. Though she managed to hang onto her weapon, something heavy bounced off it and sailed into the wall of the chamber. She glanced over to see it was an iron dagger. When she looked up the statues started coming at her, their iron feet pounding the stone floor.

Running out of the chamber, Jenna didn't bother to look back. She got across the hall and flung herself into the outer passage, diving behind the wall just as a hail of blades flew through the opening. One sliced through the outside of her arm, cutting through her sleeve and gashing her flesh.

Quickly she shifted into ghost form, and passed through another wall, emerging in the outer ward. From there she ran toward the gap in the wall where she had entered the ruins. She had to get to Domnall and the men and warn them before the iron army escaped the castle.

She nearly ran smack into her lover as she jumped over the fallen stones. He tried to catch her, but his hands passed through her arms, making her realize she was still a wraith.

He appeared just as shocked. "Jenna, why did you go in there? Why did you change?"

"I did something really stupid," she said as she took on solid form, and grabbed his hand. "But we need to run. Right now."

Chapter Twenty-Nine

As he saw the first of the iron warriors batter its way through the stone wall, Domnall snatched Jenna off her feet and ran. She clung to him as he shouted for his men, who came running from the camp to intercept them. All four stumbled to a stop and stared past him before they drew their swords.

"Scatter and climb," Domnall shouted, dispersing them.

He could hear the pounding, grating footsteps of the iron men drawing closer, and stopped at the first tree with branches sturdy enough to support his weight and hers. He jumped, catching one over his head and swung up with her.

A sword smashed into the tree just below his boots.

Pushing her higher, Domnall took in the flood of warriors still marching out of the ruins. More than a hundred now, they began clustering around the trees where his men had climbed. As he'd suspected the iron men proved too heavy to follow. The few that tried broke the lower branches with their weight and fell.

The warriors went still, and then in unison began striking the trees with their swords. Huge chips of wood began flying as they hacked into the trunks.

"'Tis a storm coming," Broden shouted to him. "I'll run for the horses."

Domnall peered up at the darkening sky. "Stay there," he shouted back. "'Tis for me to do."

"No," Jenna said. "They'll kill you the moment you're in reach."

As the tree shook beneath his grip, Domnall dropped down low enough to kick one of the iron warriors in the face. The thing fell backward and writhed on the ground, unable to rise until two others dragged it upright. Then it went still and didn't move again.

"'Tis the moss," Edane shouted from his perch in an oak tree.

Domnall looked at the unmoving iron man, who no longer sported any green on his head. The archer was right.

"Kiaran," Domnall shouted, "we need your friends."

The falconer let out a high, sharp whistle, and his kestrels dove at the warriors, snatching at the moss atop their heads. As soon as they removed it the iron man became a statue. The birds artfully dodged the swords swung at them as they did their work, until they had bared every iron head. Only when the entire army stood motionless did Domnall drop down and shove one of the statues over. It clattered to the ground like the lump of metal it was.

"Gods blind me." Mael dropped down and crouched by one of the warriors. "They attacked as if alive and thinking."

"Likely enchanted," Domnall said and looked up at Jenna, relieved that she was safe. "That 'twas a very stupit something, Wife."

"I know." She climbed down, smiling wanly as he caught her and lowered her the last few feet. "I followed some gems into the ruins, and found the statues standing in a room filled with weapons. I think it was an armory." Before he could speak, she held up her hands. "You win. This place is too dangerous for us. Let's get out of here."

A hard bang drew everyone's attention to Edane, who crouched rapping the hilt of his blade against the chest of one of the warriors. "'Tisnae hollow, Chieftain. I reckon they're solid iron."

"Aye, and I'm grateful for it. Any lighter and they'd have come up the trees." Domnall put his arm around his lover. "Gather the mounts, lads. I need but a moment with my lady."

"Before you yell at me, look at these." Jenna pulled several sparkling gems from her pocket, and placed them in his hands. "We can use them to build our home. There's also a huge diamond that I left behind near the armory." She met his gaze. "And of course we're going to leave it there, so forget I said anything about it."

"Diamonds mean naught to me." He drew her close. "I love you, Jenna."

She flung her arms around his neck, standing on her toes to kiss him. Her laughter parted their lips as he swept her off her feet and whirled her. When he put her back down, she picked up one of the warriors' swords and presented it to him with a flourish.

"You should have a battle trophy," she told him. "And whenever I don't listen to you, you can swat me with it."

"I'll but hang it where you may ever see it," Domnall said. "Mayhap over our bed."

Jenna pulled the blade back. "Well, in that case, you're going to have to work for it." She trotted off toward the camp.

Domnall smiled as he went after her, and then a bolt of white lightning came down. It blasted Jenna into the air as a deafening boom shook the ruins. His joy turned to terror as he shouted her name and ran, only to be knocked off his feet by another jagged blast.

Rolling onto his back, Domnall looked up and saw the radiant winged demon spiraling down toward him from a mass of black clouds. The Sluath flung his hand up into the blackness, and then threw another bolt down, this time directed toward his hunters.

The world smeared around Domnall as he raced over to Jenna, who lay unmoving. When he turned her over he bit back a groan. Burns shaped like fern fronds covered one side of her face, while a terrible blackened wound marred the soft skin of her throat. Smoke rose from the bottom of her boots. He touched her throat, hoping the Gods would show her mercy, but felt nothing. Her heart had stopped.

She's gone from me.

Rising to his feet, Domnall looked up at the Sluath, who had turned his attention back to him. The demon grinned at Jenna before he tossed another bolt down. Domnall seized the sword as he raced across the grass, vaulting onto the back of his mount and galloping into the air. He circled around the Sluath as it turned to pursue him, and then sharply doubled back. With every ounce of his fury he drove the iron blade at the demon.

The sword skewered the Sluath, who uttered a keening wail before dropping from the sky to flop on the ground. Quickly

Domnall guided his mount down, and reached the demon while it yet lived. He took hold of the sword, yanking it from the creature's gut.

"Where hide the rest of your horde?"

The Sluath gazed up at him looking perplexed for a moment. When he spoke, thick black fluid trickled from his mouth.

"Nowhere. Everywhere." He uttered a sound like a wet chuckle. "Inside—"

More strange blood welled up from his throat, silencing him, and then the demon's eyes emptied.

The hunters came to stand with him and watch the Sluath die. It did not go limp and unmoving like a human, but shrank and withered, its radiance extinguished, its beauty turned to hideous rot. The body continued to contract and decay until all that remained was a twisted lump of mottled ruin.

"That sword, 'tis pure iron," Edane muttered. "And we thought them unassailable."

"Burn it." Domnall turned away and went back to his dead wife, falling to his knees.

Jenna stared up at a sky she could no longer see, her eyes reflecting the thinning clouds. The Sluath had killed her, but not her beauty. He stretched out beside her, taking her cool, still hand in his.

"You promised to go nowhere without me." He brushed back the hair that had fallen across her face, taking care with each lock. "Now you're beyond me, truly. I ken that I cannae go on without you."

The world Jenna no longer walked dwindled around them.

⁂

As JENNA TURNED to the other slaves, she found Rosealise striding toward her. Deep furrows marked her forehead and dark circles underlined her eyes. But the intensity of her gaze held Jenna fast. The Englishwoman grasped her hands.

"You're sure about it then?"

Jenna wished she could muster a brave smile, but she couldn't. "I've never been more unsure of anything in my life." Her gaze swept over the other slaves. "But this has to end."

From beyond the confines of their latest cell came more shrieks of fear and cries of pain, until wild laughter roared above the clamor. Rosealise winced at the sound of the infernal braying they'd all come to know too well. Jenna squeezed the Englishwoman's hands.

"We must fight them," Jenna said. "There's no other way."

Rosealise gave her a lopsided smile. "Then we'll jolly well have to do it, won't we." She glanced behind her and saw the other slaves nodding, then nodded herself. "Right. We're with you."

"The answer is at Dun Chaill," Jenna said. "You must remember."

The cell door opened and Domnall stood holding out his hand. "'Tis time, lass."

DOMNALL FELT Jenna's grip on his hand tighten as they came out of the passage and walked onto the sky bridge. The summoned storm enveloped them in wild darkness, the enormous clouds billowing on every side. Lightning streaked over and under them, white and cold and merciless.

He turned to face her.

Knowing it might be the last time he ever beheld her, he looked his fill. The Sluath had dressed her in their strange linens woven of light. It made her appear as they did, glowing and magnificent, but her beauty was not trickery. She would forever be the loveliest thing he'd ever beheld.

"You're my heart," he said, bringing her hand to rest against his chest. "I love you. Remember that, *luaidh*."

"You said *you*, not ye. I've corrupted you." Her lips trembled as she gently stroked her fingers over one of his many wounds. "I don't know if I can do this." She met his gaze. "We could go together. We could try."

Domnall wanted nothing more than that, but they had been warned. "'Twould end us, lass."

"I'd rather die than…" She stopped and closed her eyes. "Please. Don't make me go."

"You cannae stay."

He pulled her into his arms, bathing them both in the light of her Sluath gown. He understood how she felt, for he never wished to let her go again. He'd rather die than be parted from her forever.

A tall cloaked figure rose up from the clouds, and took hold of Jenna, pulling her away. "No more time. They're waking. You must make the jump now. *Jenna.*"

She nodded, and uttered a sob. "Domnall, I love you. I'll never forget."

It took but a heartbeat. One moment Jenna was there, and then the cloaked demon touched her brow. Her eyes closed, and she vanished into the stream.

He dropped to his knees, his hands knotting against his temples, the pain tearing through him beyond anything he'd imagined. It was as if she'd wrenched his heart from his chest.

The cloaked demon hovered over him. "Now you, Mag Raith."

Slowly he got to his feet, broken and defeated as he had never been. "I'll never see her again."

"That 'tis in the hands of the Gods." The demon reached out to him. "Forgive me, Brother."

He felt the cold hand on his brow, and the

agony of losing Jenna slipped away, along with every other thought of his love. When he fell at last into the stream, he felt nothing at all.

"Chieftain."

Domnall looked up to see Broden standing over him. The memory of saying good-bye to Jenna made sense of the fragmented vision they'd shared in his cottage back in the enchanted forest. It didn't ease the rending despair of losing her again, this time to death, but it made him rise from her side. As Sluath slaves they had found love together. Once freed, they had found each other and loved again.

It had to mean something.

"We burned that facking *skeg* to ash." The trapper looked down at Jenna with true sorrow in his eyes. "We should attend now to your lady."

Domnall nodded. He couldn't leave her here, where animals would tear at her. Nor could he bear the thought of putting her in the ground. He bent and lifted her into his arms, holding her close as he tried to think. His gaze kept straying to the tumbled walls of the ruins.

Take her inside. 'Tis where she would wish to rest.

Broden kept pace with him as Domnall walked toward Dun Chaill. "Edane gathered some of the moss Kiaran's birds snatched from the iron warriors. 'Twas bespelled, but with magic of a kind he doesnae ken."

"Bid him wash his hands," Domnall said dully.

He stepped over the gap in the outer wall and carried Jenna into the passage. Walking through the twists and turns of the ruins, he found his way to the great hall she had described. He carried her to the very center of the room, where he gently placed her on the ground and closed her eyes. He would bring in more stones to cover her body and keep her safe.

Here she would always be part of their story.

But Domnall couldn't leave her alone, and waited for the men to come and join him. They would all have kind words to say. He would endure them, for he loved his brothers of the hunt almost as much as Jenna. He would leave her in their care. Then he would build from the fallen stones a tomb for her body, and his own heart.

He shut his burning eyes and slowly bowed his head.

Never had his immortality seemed more—

"Domnall?"

Chapter Thirty

✤

As Galan stabled his mount for the night in town, his thoughts returned again to the Sluath. If the legends were true, and he now suspected much of them were, the creatures could never take him. He'd kept himself inviolate. He had not shed a drop of blood in Wachvale. He would not have hurt the old crone, and she had deliberately ended herself. As long as he remained devoted to the Gods as a druid, he was untouchable. The demons might kill him, of course, but he would simply reincarnate.

He went up to his dingy room, where he created a spell circle on the pitted, stained floor. In the center he placed his traveling stele, and crowned it with a particularly rare crystal that helped him gather and restore his own power. To find the Mag Raith before Prince Iolar lost patience with him, he would need to do this nightly.

Galan carefully cleansed before he stepped into the circle and prostrated himself. Yet before he could begin to beseech the Gods, all of the candles in the room abruptly extinguished, plunging him into darkness. He sighed and rose, going to close the window but finding it already latched.

Frowning, he turned around and squinted, raising his hand against a blinding light. Through his fingers he watched his precious crystal pulsing with power, as if it were soaking up every possible source within miles. Yet he had not yet channeled his magic into it, so what could be—

"*No.*"

Galan rushed forward, only to stumble back as the crystal shattered, scattering itself beyond the confines of the circle. All of the candles in the room flared back to life.

Such a thing happened only when the

Gods had grown deeply displeased with a druid. He knew he should fall to his knees, and beg forgiveness for whatever transgression he had committed. But he had done no wrong.

Galan walked up to the spell circle, his boots crunching on the shards of his ruined crystal. In all of his lifetimes he had carefully skirted this moment, but now that it had come, he felt almost happy.

The Gods had sent a very clear message, and now it was time he did the same.

"I shall bring Fiana back to the mortal realm," he said, his hands curling into fists. "I too shall learn the secret of immortality, so that we might dwell forever together. 'Tis the only justice for our suffering."

The candles remained lit and steady. The shadows hemmed the walls of the room.

Enraged, he kicked over the stele. "You now turn against me? Then I must do the same to you. I refuse your blessings. I'll never again bow before you. You hold no more dominion over me."

Before Galan retired for the night, he tore off his robes and left them on the floor.

Tomorrow he would buy garments more suited to what he had become: a hunter of hunters.

And when he found the Mag Raith, he would have all the prey he'd ever desire.

Chapter Thirty-One

Domnall couldn't believe his ears or his eyes. The sound of Jenna's voice echoed through the great hall, clear as a bell. A light breeze rushed through the doors and arches, dancing around the man standing frozen over her. He watched the burns on her face and neck begin to shrink and disappear. She was healing. It was everything impossible.

Jenna opened her eyes to look back at him, and they seemed as bright and beautiful as ever. As she tried to sit up, he fell down beside her, and she had to grab him to keep him from toppling over.

"Hey." She laughed as he hauled her

against him. "What happened? How did I get back in here?"

"I carried you. The Sluath…the lightning…oh, lass." He kissed her mouth and her brow and held her tightly.

"Now I can't breathe," she said, her voice muffled by his tunic. "Domnall, what's going on?"

His voice shook as he drew back and told her everything. How they had escaped the Sluath, the love they had shared, the terrible choice they had made to escape and survive. By the time he explained what the demon had done Jenna's hands clutched him just as tightly.

"But I don't feel any burns," she said as she touched her face and neck. "Maybe I wasn't hurt that badly. I'm sure I was asleep and dreaming, not dead."

"Your heart stopped. But now you heal as we do." Domnall caressed her unmarked cheek. "I think you've become like us, lass."

"I died and turned into an immortal? Seems a bit extreme, but okay." Her gaze shifted, and she tugged up his sleeve. "Look what happened to your ink."

When he glanced down and saw it had turned to a gleaming gold, he lifted the back of her tunic to expose her ink. The glyphs marking her spine had changed to the same brilliant color.

A shocked cry startled them both as Mael staggered in, his eyes huge.

Jenna waved at him. "It's okay. I'm not dead anymore."

The tracker approached her as he might a wounded animal, his hands trembling and his mouth still sagging open. "I cannae believe it." He regarded Domnall. "How did you this?"

"'Twas no' my doing." But even as the words left him, he recalled his strange compulsion to carry his lady inside the ruins. "I think 'twas Dun Chaill."

"The castle brought the lass back from the dead?" That came from Edane, who led Broden and Kiaran into the hall. They moved to form a loose circle around Jenna and Domnall. "I dinnae think it could, Chieftain."

"It sent after us an army of iron warriors. It tried to drown us by waterfall. Aye, and mayhap it stole one hundred years of our lives before it handed us to the Sluath." He moved his shoulders. "I shallnae check the teeth of such a horse."

"We must go quickly," Kiaran said, and when everyone looked at him he added, "The Sluath shall come for us here now."

"'Twas only the one demon," Mael countered. "It's burnt to ash. Mayhap 'twas some manner of scout, sent to search for us."

Before Domnall could reply Jenna said, "We can't leave Dun Chaill yet." She climbed off his lap, accepting Mael's hand as she stood. "When I was, ah, dead, more of my memories came back to me." She looked at Domnall. "You took me to the sky bridge."

"Aye," Domnall said. "I remember it. 'Tis how we escaped. The underworld and this world, the two are connected by a kind of storm. The Sluath use it to move back and forth, and also through time." He dimly recalled the cloaked demon. "Someone helped free us."

"We have to find a way to cut the connection," Jenna said, the words coming faster. "We have to seal off the underworld. That way the Sluath won't ever again be able to take people and make them slaves."

Mael nodded. "And how do we that, lass?"

"I don't know, but it's here, somewhere here, in Dun Chaill." She gestured around them. "We were supposed to come here and search for it." She hesitated but then plunged on. "It wasn't just the Mag Raith and me. I remember other slaves escaping with us. There are more coming."

Every word she said rang true to him, but Domnall put his hands on her shoulders. "You're certain?"

She smiled at him. "Oh, yes."

Chapter Thirty-Two

Returning to find the hunters building a more permanent camp gratified Cul almost as much as smelling the death of one of the demons in the air. He noticed the iron warriors, now standing immobile outside the outer wall, and the damage they'd done to the trees. Dun Chaill had unleashed but a tiny part of its wrath on the intruders, and yet they had survived. It would be amusing to see how much longer they could.

He'd give them a moon, perhaps two, before they sprang a trap they couldn't defeat.

Cul retreated through the tunnels to the lower levels, and stored away the foods he had taken from Wachvale before he went to one of the listening tubes. He had placed that particular one to hear anything that approached the outside of the ruins, but it also allowed him to eavesdrop on his unwelcome guests. He took a moment to breathe in the scent of their fire on the cool air of the night, and then put the tube up to his misshapen ear.

"I think we can rebuild part of the upper level," the female was saying. "The towers are probably too unstable, but all the interior support walls in the great hall, the armory, and the granary are intact."

She's changed, Cul thought, sniffing the air that came through the tube. He felt glad for the little female. She had more spine that all five of the men put together.

"What of the trees occupying them, Jenna?" the archer asked her. "Do we build around their roots and trunks?"

Jenna. Cul let her name roll through his thoughts, enjoying the elegance of it.

"I think we should leave them where they are," she told him. "They're part of the castle now, and we can incorporate– We can find different uses for them."

"I dinnae wish to sleep in them," the bad-tempered trapper grumbled. "Keeping watch from a tree blind, 'tis wretched enough."

On and on they talked, making their plans without any true notion of what Dun Chaill was. Cul found it tedious, until the one they called chieftain said something that proved they were not quite as foolish as he'd assumed.

"We'll gather all the iron swords and daggers, and carry at least two with us," he said to his men. "If the Sluath attack again, we'll end as many as we can."

They know how to kill them.

Cul usually hated the guttural sound of his own laughter, but this revelation made him indulge in it for a long, long time.

Chapter Thirty-Three

Far beyond the mortal realm, Prince Iolar drummed his fingers against his cheek as Danar droned on about the scouts they had sent out to search for the rebels. The only satisfying moment of the day had come with Aedth's summons, and the profusion of delectably evil mortals awaiting him. He'd fed so well at the village he wouldn't have to again for weeks. He wouldn't wait that long, however.

As prince he had to keep up his strength.

"Jaeg went off to the south," Danar was saying. "But he didn't return with the others. He may have sheltered for the night for a promising cull."

"Why would he?" Iolar smothered a yawn. "He's been collecting so many new slaves lately he's run out of cages for them. He hasn't even finished marking them all."

Danar ducked his head. "I'll summon him as soon as the stream reforms."

"Use a portal, go back and find him." Iolar flicked his claws at the big *deanhan*, who hastily retreated.

The underworld had neither night nor day, but the Sluath had long ago adapted to living without the visible passage of time. After hearing the latest reports Iolar would usually spend several hours alone with his treasure. Reveling in its many delights kept him from over-indulging in other, less beneficial pursuits. Only the rebels had taken his treasure from him when they'd fled. Without knowing the exact moment his treasure had been swept off to the mortal realm, Iolar had little hope of recovering it.

He snapped his fingers, cutting his own flesh, and licked the bead of black blood from his skin as two of his personal guards presented themselves.

"Bring me a male and a female," he told them. "Not too old, and check first to see that they're not addled."

"Do you wish them clothed, naked, bloodied or fresh?" one of the guards asked.

"Clothed and fresh," he said. "I'm in the mood for some sport. Oh, and be sure they've not been claimed yet."

As the prince expected the male lasted far longer than the female, and even tried to protect her from him. The entertainment they offered, however, soon palled. Unable to abide the monotony, he sent them to be tormented to death.

Danar came to him as soon as he returned from the mortal realm, and the moment Iolar saw his face he knew what news he brought.

"Jaeg is gone," the prince said. As the *deamhan* nodded, Iolar surged to his feet. "Killed by the hands of mortals? How can this be? Who killed him?"

"I cannot tell you, but when I tasted his death," the big demon said, "it burned of iron."

Iolar was no longer bored. "*Iron*," he said

through clenched teeth. His narrowed eyes glanced around the room. "Then it seems we have a traitor amongst us."

Chapter Thirty-Four

Jenna sat back against Domnall's chest and watched the last of the campfire flames flickering low. The rest of the men had gone off to sleep, but she felt like running a few laps around the ruins. If all this energy was a side effect of the immortality, which she still wasn't sure she believed, then she'd definitely keep it.

"Getting struck by lightning should feel awful, but I'm great. I'm not even tired," she told her lover. "Maybe I should run around waving a sword in every thunderstorm."

He rested his chin on the top of her head. "Then I shall take back my vow no' to beat you."

"Too late for that." A smug smile tilted her

lips. "You've fallen in love with me twice, and the second time you didn't remember a thing about me. If that's not meant to be, then it has to involve magic. Resign yourself to the fact that you're putty in my hands, Chieftain."

"'Tis likely why I agreed to stay here," he said, sounding grumpy now.

"We just have to be careful, and clear all the spaces for traps before we start rebuilding and moving in." She turned around to face him, excitement brightening her eyes. "This could become our home, Domnall. We could have a life here."

"Many lives." He kissed her brow. "As long as you stay with me, my lady, you may have whatever you wish, within reason." He looked into her eyes. "But leave the iron swords and thunderstorms to us."

Jenna laughed. "There's something else I should mention about us escaping the under-world. I'm not sure I should tell the men because, well, it took you and me thirteen centuries to find each other. I'll let you make that decision."

He frowned. "What did you recall?"

"The other slaves who escaped with us."

She glanced out at the sleeping hunters. "They were all female."

Domnall sighed. "Dinnae tell me they were with my men as you and I were."

"I don't remember that much," she admitted. "But they were all willing to fight the Sluath, and they're all coming here, to Dun Chaill." She snuggled against him. "So that's everything I know. We'll just have to see who turns up."

"'Tis one more thing I must tell you, lass," Domnall said gently, and leaned down to whisper it in her ear.

Jenna smacked his arm lightly. "I know you can move faster than sound, but honestly. There's no way horses can fly."

Sneak Peek

Mael (Immortal Highlander, Clan Mag Raith Book 2)

Excerpt

CHAPTER ONE

Temptation, Mael mag Raith realized that morning, made a man wholly dolt-headed.

The unusually warm spring in Scotland had festooned Dun Chaill in flowery vines and ample shade from the flourishing trees. Moss now so thickly carpeted the forest surrounding the castle ruins it had begun creeping up the tumble-down stonework. Daily washed by lavish morning dew, the air smelled like a coddled maiden, soft and sweetly fragrant.

After laboring for weeks to make habitable the intact portion of Dun Chaill's keepe, Mael had quickly agreed to help his chieftain reclaim the kitchen garden. While he had no skill with planting, all of the men had tired of foraging in the sprawling forests. Soon they would need more to add to their limited food sources. The prospect of working outdoors had cheered him as well, for how hard could it prove?

What he should have done, Mael thought as he stood buried to the hips in greenery gone wild, was first have a look at the *bourach*.

"'Tis hopeless, Chieftain," Mael said, grimacing as he pried a spiky thistle from his sleeve. "I say we burn and plant anew."

"You'll tell Jenna she cannae have fresh strewings until the solstice," Domnall mag Raith said as he waded through a white-spangled snarl of hawthorn and meadowsweet. Standing almost as tall and broad as the tracker, the chieftain looked just as incongruous. "Then bid Edane seek elsewhere wood sorrel for his tonics, and Broden sweet berries for his snares."

"I'd rather beg the Gods smite me." Mael eyed a patch of sky. "Why didnae I remain in the hall to muck out the hearths? 'Tis humble work, and yet can be finished well before the snows arrive. This?" He shook his head.

"'Tis no' so bad. 'Twill need but taming and tending." Domnall surveyed the unculti-vated growth around them. "We should ken the range of what may be saved."

"I'll trodge to the back." Mael peered over a snarled spread of purple blooms before glancing down at the hundreds of pods they'd sprouted. "'Twould seem we willnae want for seed, but I reckon I'd rather eat dirt."

The chieftain grunted. "'Tis good horse fodder, vetch." He reached down and plucked a blushing rose from the undergrowth, a rare smile lighting up his tough features. "We must save some flowers for my lady."

Pushing through the tall grasses until he cleared them, Mael tried to stave off the familiar stab of envy. Since mating with Jenna Cameron, Domnall's nature had vastly changed. He no longer retreated into icy indifference and bleak silences. While they all labored in various ways to improve their situation, the chieftain had worked tirelessly to transform the abandoned stronghold. He meant to make it a true home for his wife and his men. Mael had no doubt that all of it sprang from the deep, abiding love Domnall had found with Jenna.

'Tis their reward for all they've endured, this life they build.

Mael had no illusions about his own future. He'd inherited his sire's massive build and outlandish strength, and looked every inch a brute. While some females regarded his size as proof of his virility, none could gaze upon him without a shiver. The lasses of his tribe thought him the same as defender Fargus mag Raith, who had nightly vented his endless rage on his mate and bairns.

Unlike his sire Mael had always been of a mild, thoughtful temperament. Indeed, he'd often thought it a punishment from the Gods for pairing his cherishing nature with such a fearsome appearance.

Beyond the vetch he found wild carrots and turnips paving the ground with lacy cups and broad fronds of green. The plentiful roots would add flavor to their pottages, and even feed the mounts when grazing grew thin in the cold season. Yet when Mael lifted his gaze he saw they had crept out from under an unkempt hedge of juniper that stretched in an enormous curve that seemed to have no end. Even more puzzling, behind it he could see the top of a wych elm hedge and another of blackthorn growing behind it.

"Chieftain," he called to Domnall as he looked down the long wall of spiky leaves and berries. "We've more than we reckoned back here."

#

"It looks to me like an overgrown hedge maze," Jenna Cameron said that night as they gathered in the hall for the evening meal. She passed a platter of oatcakes to her mate before she saw the blank looks the rest of the men were giving her. "That's a garden labyrinth made from shrubs or small trees trimmed to serve as walls. But they date back only as far as the Renaissance—ah, the mid-sixteenth century—so I'm probably wrong."

Mael didn't doubt her, but something

about the carefully planted hedges set his teeth on edge. "And if you're no', lass?"

"'Twas likely meant to catch and end the unwary, like every other facking thing in this place," said Broden, his handsome face set in its habitual scowl. "No matter what 'tis, we should burn it."

Gleaming red braids bobbed as their archer, Edane, nodded. "Aye, spread flames in the midst of all that deadfall and blowdown. We'll clear at least the forest and the ruins before the smoke summons the Sluath to descend on us."

"Let them come." The trapper drove his eating dagger into the top of the trestle table. "We ken how to kill them now."

Kiaran dragged a hand through his red-gold mane, making the kestrel on his shoulder fly off to join the other trained raptors perched in the rafters. "We're five against a horde of demons. Aye, surely we'll prevail."

"Enough," Domnall said before the men could start arguing in earnest. He met Mael's gaze. "As seneschal the grounds as well as the stronghold shall be your domain. What say you?"

The tracker felt a little startled to be given the position as well as the say, but it seemed sensible. Since boyhood he'd shared the work of his *máthair* and sisters, and had the nature best suited to managing this unruly household.

"'Tisnae a present threat to us," Mael said after giving it more thought. "I'd clear the garden first. Take stock of the maze after, and learn if 'tis safe or no'."

Broden snatched up his food, mumbled something like an apology to Jenna, and stalked out.

Edane made a rude sound, caught Domnall's eye, and then turned his attention to his trencher.

After they finished the meal, Domnall lingered to help Mael bank the hearth and take apart the trestle table, which when not in use they hung on wall hooks.

"I might have first asked you to serve as my seneschal," he said.

"You never ask, for you're never wrong." Mael grinned at him. "'Tis facking annoying. Dinnae keep your lady waiting so you might smooth my feathers. You plucked them all long ago."

"Still, Brother." The chieftain inclined his head. "My thanks."

Mael watched him stride off in the direction of the chamber he shared with Jenna. The thought of seeking his own empty bed didn't appeal to him, so he took down a torch. There weren't enough of them to stand regular sentry, but he could patrol once around the ruins. It might tire him out, and keep him from staring at the wall cracks for half the night.

Outside the great hall he navigated from memory the warren of dark, cluttered passages until he stepped over the rubble of the inner ward's back wall. Beyond it lay the front of the wild garden. He and Domnall had cleared a narrow foot trail, down which a sudden, chilly wind now blew. It brought with it a booming sound, like echoed thunder from the ridges, as well as a strange, stuttering, metallic noise. Holding his torch aloft shed light on nothing new, so Mael started down the path.

#

The wind buffeted Rosealise Dashlock with the fervor of its intent on flaying her to the bone. Yet even as she whirled and tumbled through the air, she felt gladdened. The pale curls lashing her face could be brushed and pinned. Her limbs, now no longer limp and leaden, felt very strong indeed. As soon as she found some footing and a handhold, she would defeat this wretched gale, and then she would...

...and then she would...

There had to be something she would do. Rosealise simply couldn't think of it for the buffeting and twirling.

The clouds below her parted, revealing a flaring flame, a silhouette of an enormous figure, and a huge web of shadows surrounding both. Instinctively she flipped away from the fire, falling squarely atop the figure beside it, which collapsed beneath her. The fire fell away, illuminating the face of a very large man. He stared at her, his topaz eyes wide, and then promptly swooned.

"Such an abominable denouement." She pushed herself up from his very broad chest and felt his rough shirt graze her breasts—her bare breasts, she saw as she glanced down.

"Hello? Sir? Good gracious, have I killed you?"

The large man said nothing, but she rose an inch as he took a breath.

"Thank heavens." Rosealise struggled upright. In addition to straddling the large man in a most inappropriate manner, she hadn't a stitch of clothing on her tall, pale body. She regarded the man's primitive-looking tunic, which she still clutched with both hands. "Sir, forgive me, but…might I borrow this?"

• • • • •

Buy *Mael (Immortal Highlander, Clan Mag Raith Book 1)*

MORE BOOKS BY HH

For a complete, up-to-date book list, visit
HazelHunter.com/books.

Get notifications of new releases and special
promotions by joining my newsletter!

Glossary

Here are some brief definitions to help you navigate the medieval world of the Clan Mag Raith series.

aulden: medieval slang for archaic

bairn: child

bannock: a round, flat loaf of unleavened Scottish bread

bloodwort: alternate name for yarrow

borage: alternate name for starflower (Borago officinalis)

broch: an ancient round hollow-walled structure found only in Scotland

burraidh: Scots Gaelic for "bully"

cac: Scots gaelic for "shit"

conclave: druid ruling body

Cornovii: name by which two, or three, tribes
were known in Roman Britain

cottar: an agricultural worker or tenant given
lodgings in return for work

Cuingealach: Scots Gaelic for "the narrow pass"

deamhan (plural: deamhanan): Scots Gaelic
for demon

doss: leaves, moss, and other detritus covering
the ground

dru-wid: Proto Celtic word; an early form
of "druid"

drystane: a construction of stacked stone or
rock that is not mortared together

fash: feel upset or worried

grice: a breed of swine found in the Highlands
and Islands of Scotland and in Ireland

groat: a type of medieval silver coin worth
approximately four pence

gu bràth: Scots Gaelic for forever, or until
Judgment

hold your wheesht: Scottish slang term for
maintaining silence and calm

hoor: medieval slang for whore, prostitute

jess: a short leather strap that is fastened
around each leg of a hawk

kirk: Scottish slang for church

kithan: Medieval Scots term for a demon

luaidh: Scots Gaelic for "loved one" or "darling"

maister: medieval slang for master or leader

máthair: Scots Gaelic for "mother"

nag: slang for horse

naught-man: an unearthly creature that only looks like a man

nock: the slotted end of an arrow that holds it in place on the bowstring

panay: alternate name for self-heal (Prunella vulgaris)

parti: the ideas or plans influencing an architect's design

peridot: a green semi-precious mineral, a variety of olivine.

rooing: removing sheep's loose fleece by hand-pulling

skeg: Scots Gaelic for "demon"

stand hunt: to watch for prey from a blind or place of concealment

stele: an upright pillar bearing inscriptions

stockman: a person who looks after livestock

tapachd: Scots Gaelic for "an ability of confi-

dent character not to be afraid or easily
intimidated"
taverit: Scottish slang for worn out, exhausted
trigging: in stonework, using wedge pieces to
secure a construct
woundwort: alternate name for wound healer
(Anthyllis vulneraria)

Pronunciation Guide

A selection of the more challenging words in the Immortal Highlander, Clan Mag Raith series.

Aklen: ACK-lin
bannock: BAN-ick
Broden mag Raith: BRO-din MAG RAYTH
burraidh: BURR-ee
cac: kak
Carac: CARE-ick
Clamhan: CLEM-en
Cornovii: core-KNOW-vee-eye
Cuingealach: kwin-GILL-ock
Cul: CULL
Danar: dah-NAH
Darro: DAR-oh

deamhan: DEE-man

Domnall mag Raith: DOM-nall
MAG RAYTH

Dun Chaill: DOON CHAYLE

Eara: EER-ah

Edane mag Raith: eh-DAYN MAG RAYTH

Fargas: FAR-gus

Fiana: FEYE-eh-nah

Fraser: FRAY-zir

Galan Aedth: gal-AHN EEDTH

groat: GROWT

gu bràth: GOO BRATH

Hal Maxwell: HOWL MACK-swell

Iolar: EYE-el-er

Jaeg: YEGG

Jenna Cameron: JEHN-nah CAM-er-ahn

Kiaran mag Raith: KEER-ahn MAG RAYTH

kithan: KEY-tin

luaidh: LOO-ee

Lyle Gordon: lie-EL GORE-din

Mael mag Raith: MAIL MAG RAYTH

marster: MAR-stir

máthair: muh-THERE

Meirneal: MEER-nee-el

Nectan: NECK-tin

parti: PAR-tee

Rodney Percell: RAHD-knee purr-SELL

Seabhag: SHAH-vock

Sileas: SIGH-lee-ess

skeg: SKEHG

Sluath: SLEW-ahth

tapachd: TAH-peed

taverit: tah-VAIR-eet

Wachvale: WATCH-veil

wheesht: WEESHT

Dedication

For Mr. H.

Copyright

Copyright © 2019 Hazel Hunter

This is a work of fiction. Names, characters, places, and incidents are products of the author's imagination or are used fictitiously and are not to be construed as real. Any resemblance to actual events, locales, organizations, or persons, living or dead, is coincidental.

All rights reserved. No part of this book may be used or reproduced in any manner, stored in or introduced into a retrieval system, or transmitted, in any form, or by any means (electronic, mechanical, photocopying, recording, or otherwise), without the prior written consent of the copyright owner.

The scanning, uploading, and distribution of this book via the Internet or via any other means without the permission of the copyright owner is illegal. Please purchase only authorized electronic editions, and do not participate in or encourage electronic piracy of copyrighted materials. Your support of the author's rights is appreciated.

Made in the USA
Las Vegas, NV
16 February 2021

17919484R00213